Kate's eyes blazed; her tone was bitter. "It seems the freetraders place their faith on a frail rock. I surmise you were so enthralled by this—this creature's charms that you forgot all else."

Suddenly, studying his face, she saw her words were true. "Richard, can you not see? She is but using you to try to wheedle information out of you."

"You are scarcely flattering. Does it not occur to you that she may regard me—in another light?"

For a long moment she looked at him. Then, "Yes, I have assumed too much. Already she has spun her web for you."

"It is you who have done that, Kate. You are like a species of spider which, having drained him dry, kills her mate."

Crossing swiftly to the door, she flung it open.

"Go to her! Make a fool of her as you have of me, with your easy promises, your sudden embraces. But doubtless she is cleverer than I. She will have your ring on her finger before *she* reveals the secrets of her heart. . . ."

Also by the author:*

THE SPANISH DOLL
PRELUDE TO LOVE

THE
GENEROUS VINE
ELIZABETH RENIER

ACE BOOKS

A Division of Charter Communications Inc.
1120 Avenue of the Americas
New York, N. Y. 10036

To

NORREY FORD

with gratitude and affection

I should like to acknowledge my thanks to my friend Constance Cox, who so generously allowed me to call upon her wide knowledge of the customs, dress and manners of the eighteenth century

An ACE STAR Book
by arrangement with Hurst & Blackett Ltd.

Printed in the U.S.A.

1

The night, dark and hushed, pulsated with the secret stirring of the village. Stealthily, with a soft hiss and gurgle, as if in the conspiracy of silence, the sea crept along the mud-banks of the estuary. The hoot of a tawny owl, quavering, eerie, sounded from the elms above the churchyard. The slow minutes moved towards high water.

In the village, deaf and dumb on such a night, a door opened; then another. From inn and shop, stable and cottage, dark figures emerged, to disappear with wary footsteps along the road which led around the inlet.

A ragged, one-legged boy, stretched on a doorstep with his rough-hewn crutch for pillow, woke from a troubled sleep. Trembling, he drew farther back into the shadows and covered his ears with thin hands. To see nothing, hear nothing; that was the only safety on the night of a smugglers' run.

A mangy dog, searching for scraps, surprised a cat intent on a mousehole. The screech and shrill barking sent a shiver through the girl who stood, peering from the doorway of her cottage. Then she chuckled in her throat, and experienced the familiar tingle of excitement as she stepped outside and softly closed the door.

The action, symbolic, amused her. She was shutting the door not only upon the safety of her home but also upon her respectable, law-abiding daytime self—upon the Kate Hardham who ran the little dame's school and went regularly to church and was shocked that she had not yet cured Judith of stealing.

Exulting in the unrestricted movement accorded by men's clothing, she strode through the wood and along the lane to Tom Blackmore's farm. Her thoughts, with sweet anticipation, turned to Richard. At this moment he, too, would be leaving his home, riding a horse with muffled hooves down the long drive from the manor house. In her mind's eye she saw him, slim and lithe in his green, caped riding-coat; his auburn hair, curled and tied with black ribbon, beneath the cocked, three-cornered hat.

The savage cry of a hunting vixen wrenched her thoughts back to the task in hand. Tom Blackmore had said the stable door would be unlocked and he would have his head under the bedclothes, like all sensible men who were not abroad that night.

A candle flickered in the farm-house kitchen. The girl halted, stifling an exclamation of dismay. Was this unexpected light a warning?

She started as Tom's head appeared over the yard wall.

"Who's there?" he whispered.

"Kate—Kate Hardham."

"You've come for the mare?"

"Yes."

"There's a hitch. My wife's brother rode over from Emsworth. He lodges here the night. His son's a coastguard; caught two freetraders over at Cuckmere—hanged in chains, they were. 'Twill not be safe for you to take the mare this night."

"That makes two packhorses short. Jesse's pony went lame this morning."

"I'm sorry. Sorrier still in the morning, when there's no keg of spirits at my door. I must go back now. Good luck."

Kate returned along the lane, frowning. Two things had gone wrong tonight, and bad luck goes in threes, she thought. Their luck had been in for so long. There had been good cargoes, good prices, and with Sir Charles Glynde keeping the excisemen quiet, almost it had been too easy. Remembering the date, she shivered, and hurried to her rendez-vous with Richard.

She waited for him, under the elms where the rooks moved restlessly on their nests. A few twigs pattered down through the branches, like rain, as loud as pistol shots in her ears. She heard the muffled thud of hooves and went forward to meet Richard. Her strong, clear voice was modified to a soft whisper as she called his name.

He peered into the darkness under the trees, scarcely able to distinguish her figure but acutely aware of her presence.

"Kate? Why are you not mounted?"

Quickly she explained, her hand gentling his horse as it became restless at the delay.

"Two packhorses short," he repeated thoughtfully. "That means we'll need another hiding-place."

"You can stow the kegs in my loft as we used to do."

"No. I'll not have that. It took me months to wean you from such folly. Besides, you have Judith to think of now."

"Do you think I forget?" she asked indignantly. "It is partly for Judith I remain a freetrader, to help pay for her keep."

"I have told you there is no need. I would give you money gladly."

She stamped her foot on the hard ground. "And *I* have told *you* I will accept my own responsibilities. I'll not take charity, from you or anyone."

Richard sighed. "Very well. But I'll not use your loft. We'll hide the extra kegs in Nan Gunter's cellar. She looks so like a witch no Preventive man would enter *her* cottage. Give me your hand. You must ride pillion with me."

It was an effort to mount her behind him. He was lightly built and she no delicate, fine-boned creature. Her shoulders were as broad as his, rendering easy the deception of her clothes. In breeches and shirt and broadcloth coat, her thick, curling black hair imprisoned in a kerchief, two things only betrayed her womanhood—the full curve of her breasts, and the delicate wrists and hands. Her dark eyes were as bold, her nerves as steady, as any man's.

Into this one child of their marriage, her parents had distilled the essence of their two selves; the laughing recklessness of a sea captain, and the gentle patience which his wife had brought to all her tasks. Both dead, they had left within this eighteen-year-old girl a battleground which she had not yet recognised. Life to Kate was an adventure, full of promise and challenge. She found satisfaction in teaching the local children. There was always the hope that one day she would discover a child whose mind she could open to the beauty of words as hers had been opened by Richard.

The horse stumbled on the uneven road, throwing her forward against Richard. She laughed, a rich sound in her throat.

"Hush!" he warned her. "I will send you home if you make so much noise."

She laughed again, more softly. "*You* will send *me!* Do you forget that I was a freetrader a year before you joined us?"

He spoke in a tight-lipped whisper. "I have not forgotten. I would never have taken these foolhardy risks if you had not taunted me—as you taunted me all through our childhood, to climb the tallest trees or to swim across the estuary or ride that hard-mouthed brute of my father's."

She threw up her head. "You should be glad. I made a man of you."

She felt him stiffen. She laid her hand on his arm. "I should not have said that, Richard. Forgive me."

"It is true."

For she had put heart into him when there was no one else to care. Austere and withdrawn, his father had spent his days with his books or his telescope, studying the stars, regarding Richard as his mother's murderer since she had died at his birth. The Manor was silent, oppressive; his governess without love, his tutor without pity.

Remembering, he pressed Kate's fingers. "All the warmth I have ever known—all my happiness—has been with you, Kate."

She laid her cheek against his neck, sighing with contentment. But immediately she was jerked upright as Richard reined his horse.

"What was that?" he exclaimed.

"Naught but a sheep. They will be lambing without Silas this night. He has business to attend to which will pay him better than shepherding."

But despite her reassuring words, she felt uneasy.

"Richard, did you go first to Falcon Grange?"

"Of course."

"The excisemen are there—becoming stupid on Sir Charles's wine?"

"They will be under the table before another hour has passed."

She bit her lip. "You will laugh at me, I know. But it *is* the thirteenth of the month. Jesse's pony going lame; Tom Blackmore's brother-in-law choosing this day to visit—I wish a third misfortune, a very small one, would happen quickly, so that it is finished."

He did laugh at her, teasingly. "You and your superstitions! Your father has much to answer for!"

"But he was often right. About his own death, even. Think you his ship would have foundered if he had not left behind his caul—that charm against drowning which had served him so well?"

"We die when we are meant to, Kate. No talisman can alter that. For shame on you, living under the shadow of the church as you do."

"The parson does not know everything. Judith says—"

"Judith? What can a blind girl know?"

"While she was with the gipsies they taught her—"

"To beg—and steal if she could."

She sighed. "Yes, that too. But she is improving, Richard. This week 'twas but a bunch of ribbons."

He laughed at her again, and was relieved to hear her throaty chuckle. He did not relish gipsies' tales, nor superstitious forebodings, on the night of a run.

They all relied on him now, the fifty-odd of their band. Despite their strength and their roughness, they accorded him the leadership, good-humouredly tolerating his aloof "gentry" ways because they recognised the superior brain which had planned their activities so successfully for the past year. Since he joined them, they had caught neither sight nor sound of an exciseman. The Frenchman sailed into the estuary with no hindrance from the revenue cutter. The long line of laden packhorses plodded through the hollow ways of Sussex en route for London, and returned with saddlebags weighted with silver.

Through Richard they had gained the safeguard which made them almost recklessly confident—the backing of Sir Charles Glynde, the biggest and most influential landowner in the district. It had been Sir Charles's money which enabled them to buy bigger cargoes on the Continent. Along the route to London he had friends who enjoyed French brandy and whose wives appreciated fine silks and laces. In London his pleas for reform of the customs laws had been ignored. Now, a bachelor living alone, save for his servants, in the fortress-like Grange which was his ancestral home, he marshalled his forces in secret to outwit the Government. But he would have no bloodshed. The Preventive men were not to blame for Parliament's misdeeds. They were but men with their bread to earn.

There had been no bloodshed for a year. But still each man carried his weapon. Each man ordered his womenfolk to stay behind closed shutters. Richard would not allow success to beget carelessness. For the price of failure was the gibbet.

The men waited, grouped along the muddy edge

of the inlet opposite the village. Metal jingled as a horse moved restlessly. Men grunted out an oath or two. The water lapped gently against the reeds.

As Richard and Kate dismounted, the men moved closer, a dark huddle against the faintly luminous background of the sea. Richard gave his instructions about the extra loads, sent a man to warn Nan Gunter her cellar would be needed.

A redshank sprang, piping in alarm, from the rushes beside them. Richard swore softly. A ribald joke came from the back of the group. A man pointed. Every head turned seawards.

"There she is. That's the lugger's light."

Far out, over the flat waste of the estuary, the ship's lantern rode gently towards them, a strange new star in the blackness of the night.

Richard stiffened. "Silas, you have the lantern? Show them the 'All clear.'"

The shepherd, his back to the village, lifted and dropped the trap of his lantern three times. An answering triple flash came from across the water.

Richard ordered, "Into the boats. Quietly now!"

A group of men detached itself and moved to the waiting boats. The water protested with quick, plopping ripples as they shoved off. A thole-pin creaked. A misjudged oar hit the surface with a faint splash.

Kate, beside Richard, could feel his tenseness. They waited, the ponies tethered beneath the scrub oak. The cry of the tawny owl sounded eerily across the water. A wader called softly overhead. There were scrabblings and rustlings in the undergrowth; the scream of a tortured rabbit.

The light on the Frenchman's lugger went out. The boats returned, low in the water.

The band went into action, heaving the kegs and barrels on to the horses' backs, grunting with their efforts, cursing the animals which would not stand still. At a word from Richard they set off, a long procession of dark shapes. The ponies plodded patiently, heavily laden, along the uneven path, round the end of the inlet. Skirting the village, they went up a side-lane and entered the dark tunnel under the trees.

Several men left the main body. There were barrels to be delivered at the inn, silk and lace to be hidden at Nan Gunter's; brandy to be dropped off for the farmers who left their stable-doors unlocked on such a night.

The rest moved on, resolutely, with Richard at their head.

"You should not lift those heavy weights," he told Kate, walking beside him. "That is not woman's work."

She laughed defiantly. "Is any of smuggling, then, woman's work?"

"It is not. But you are not bound by women's laws, so I'll save my breath."

Women's laws, she thought, what are they? The rules that bade you sit behind a man upon a horse, cook his meals, bear his children, wait upon him, defer to him in all things, acknowledging him to be master. But that was not for her. As long as Richard understood that, they could be happy, when in due time they came to the point of marriage. Of what use to him, who had needed taking by the hand to lead him from the lonely dream-world of his books, would be a vapid, helpless girl who looked to him always for decisions?

She moved closer, seeing as they emerged from

13

the trees, the clear handsome lines of his profile, her knowledge filling in the details of auburn hair and hazel eyes, the wide and generous mouth. His boots were polished, his cravat tied as carefully as if he were attending a ball instead of leading a band of outlaws. In the past she had teased him about the elegance of his clothes, in contrast to the careless flinging on of her own. He had retaliated by grabbing a handful of her hair and telling her no man would want her to wife if she did not mend her hoydenish ways.

As she grew out of childhood she remembered his words. Now, save on these expeditions, she dressed in the full skirts and low bodices which had come into fashion in the second half of the eighteenth century and which he admired. She wore on a gold chain around her neck the cross that had been his mother's. With this he had plighted his troth to her, one summer's day amongst the roses at the Manor. She had been ten; he thirteen. His shy, uncertain kiss had landed on her ear.

Neither had mentioned the incident again. But she hugged the memory inside her, and the cross never left her neck, day or night. One day soon, she thought, he would speak again. When he came of age in the summer, he would ask her to marry him. For who else would he want to share the rest of his life but his childhood companion? Until then, she was content. The passion of love had not yet touched her; she knew only its gentleness, and was happy in the unclouded pleasure of Richard's nearness and the knowledge that he needed her.

They came to the great iron gates of the Grange, each pillar topped by a stone falcon. Richard and Kate waited while ten men passed through and led

14

their horses on to the damp grass of the park. The rest, mounted, set out on their long and secret journey, with a whispered farewell and a smothered laugh.

Always there were those who joked, and those who swore, and those who seldom talked, like Silas, the shepherd.

Richard and Kate passed through the gateway into the park. Under the trees, the beechmast crunched beneath their feet. The startled deer threw up their heads and bounded away. At the edge of the trees, the chalk of the beech hanger gleamed white.

The men halted. Silas went forward and cautiously, so that he would not send the loose stones rattling down the slope, pulled aside a thicket of brambles. Big Jesse Turner, the innkeeper, lit a lantern. Its shaded light shone into the passage behind the undergrowth.

Without a word, each man unloaded his pony and formed into line beside the thicket. With an even rhythm, the kegs were passed along until they were all stowed in the underground cave. The brambles sprang back across the entrance. The lantern was put out. The men mounted their horses and rode back towards the gate.

It was Kate who saw, through the trees, the light from the open door of the Grange. She pulled at Richard's sleeve, heard his swift indrawn breath.

"Remain where you are, every one of you, and not a sound," he ordered.

Tensely, they waited under the spreading beeches. A lantern bobbed across the courtyard. Two horses were silhouetted against the light from the hall. There followed a confusion of figures in the doorway, shouted orders, and the thud of hooves in the drive.

A startled whisper ran around the group. "The Preventive men."

"Richard, what can have gone wrong?" Kate demanded.

But he did not answer. This was the moment he had dreaded always. For a year they had been safe, unmolested. He had led them in what was no more than a secret business venture. But now . . .

Never had he really faced this possibility—that one day he might be called upon to use force, to give the order to fight. But this would be no fight. They were a dozen against two. Behind him were men who faced the gibbet or transportation if caught. At the Grange was his friend who had above all things insisted on no bloodshed.

As in a dream, he heard the clicking of the pistol hammers being drawn back. He heard Kate's voice, urgent, in his ear.

"Richard, give your orders. They are nigh on top of us."

But all he could answer was, "There is to be no shooting. I gave my word to Sir Charles."

"Are we then all to hang?" she demanded. "Give me your pistol." She wrenched it from its holster. "There may be no need to shoot. They may— Listen!"

Two voices, thick with drink, were raised in a bawdy song. The hoofbeats slowed. A few yards from the silent group a voice complained, "I've losht m' shtirrup. Hold hard, you brute, or I'll f-fall off."

A horse whinnied softly under the trees.

"Whash that?" the same voice queried.

The two men drew abreast of the smugglers. One laughed, his cackle choked by a hiccup.

"S-somebody having a joke. Or 'praps it's a ghost —Sir Charles's ghost."

Kate steadied her weapon against Richard's thigh. He knew she must be aware of the tautness of his every nerve. The beat of his heart threatened to deafen him, its pressure to burst his ribs. No situation he had ever faced, led on by the girl sitting so coolly behind him, could compare with this. Blindly he groped in his mind for some words she had uttered earlier, and it was as if she spoke them again now, confidently, expecting no denial.

"I have made a man of you."

He jerked back his shoulders, drew a long, shuddering breath. He took the pistol from her hand.

The two excisemen were still shouting, arguing in the drive. Jesse Turner moved impatiently, muttered a threat.

"Keep still," Richard whispered. "They have not scented us yet."

He could sense the tension all around him, the fingers tightening on firearm and club. There was another cackle of fuddled laughter.

The man who had first spoken announced, "I've found m' shtirrup. Funny thing, it was on my foot all the time. Le'sh be on our way. We'd best be far from here by daylight."

Their tipsy singing faded beyond the gate. A dozen sighs gusted into the night air. A dozen oaths sped the Preventive men on their way.

Kate laughed, a little uncertainly.

"So those are the dreaded Customs men. I could have cracked their heads together, and tied them up, with my bare hands."

17

Richard's brain was clear now. He said quietly, "Something is amiss. You will all wait here while I go up to the house and discover what has happened."

Muttering amongst themselves, the men moved farther back into the wood. Reaching the house, Richard left Kate to hold his horse and disappeared into the darkness beside the stables. The loneliness of the night closed around her, and its silence. Until she heard, for the third time, the unearthly hoot of the tawny owl. When it called outside a window, it was said, it had come to claim a soul. She shivered, recalling her earlier foreboding. But had they not already endured their third stroke of bad luck in the untimely appearance of the excisemen? Or was there some other, some greater misfortune, yet to come?

The horse grew restless, pawing the grass. Why was Richard so long? She did not altogether trust the men to wait indefinitely. The danger was over; they would be thinking longingly of their beds.

Richard came round the corner of the house, accompanied by a servant with a lantern. His step was slow, his face stricken in the flickering light.

Swiftly Kate went to him, took his hands. "Richard, what is it? What has happened?"

Dazedly he looked into her anxious face.

"I bring bad news for us all. Sir Charles Glynde died of a heart attack—an hour ago," he said.

2

"Then what happened?" asked Judith, standing patiently while Kate adjusted the fichu on her dress.

"Why, then we had to return and fetch out the kegs and hide them elsewhere. Richard said that many people would come to the Grange, relatives and lawyers, in the next few weeks, so that the cave in the park would not be safe."

"Where did you take the cargo?"

Kate chuckled. "Some of it is stowed in the churchyard, in the two hollow tombs against the sea wall. Parson will have a gift of brandy to ensure he does not walk that way. What he has not seen, he cannot speak of."

The blind girl laughed with her. But Kate added seriously, "I should not have told you, Judith. If there should ever be questions, you must know nothing. It would be safer for you if I had never told you what I do on certain nights."

"Since when has my life been safe?" the girl asked bitterly.

Kate tied the last ribbon and curled a soft, fair ringlet around her finger.

"I had hoped, since you came to me."

Judith flung herself into the older girl's arms. "Forgive me. I did not mean—it is just that I was so anxious, when you did not come home until morning."

"Poor child! I will not go, if it frightens you so." She held the girl tightly, feeling the fragile bones under the thin layer of flesh. The beautiful grey, sightless eyes brimmed with tears as Judith raised her head.

"You must not give up anything for me, Kate. It is enough . . . that you let me stay under your roof and care for me so . . . so tenderly."

Kate kissed the girl's pale cheek. "Why should I not? I discovered you at my door like a gift from God. A brother I found in Richard. Always I regretted the lack of a sister. But this is no time for tears. The sun is shining, and in that yellow muslin and the straw hat with the wide ribbon we bought in Chichester, you look as pretty as the primroses blooming in the hedgerows."

Judith banished her tears. Her fingers groped for the grey cloak lying on the settle.

"Am I truly pretty, Kate?"

"Truly. Do you wish me to tell you it every day —item by item? That your eyebrows curve like a skylark's wing? That your mouth is as sweet and gentle as your nature? That, when you sleep, your lashes lie upon your cheek as innocently as a child's? There, see how foolishly you make me speak with your pleading."

"I wish that I might talk as you do."

"Think you I would have so many words, so many good thoughts to cherish, if I had not had access to Richard's books, to all the treasure of the Manor library?"

"Richard has been good to you, has he not?"

Kate paused in the act of fastening her own dark cloak. "Indeed, yes. He has taught me most of the subjects with which I now earn my living. Through his friendship with Sir Charles, he gained for me my parents' cottage and the means to start my school.

But it has not been all taking, Judith. In return, I—"

How was it possible to explain what she had given to Richard, through all the years of his restricted, lonely boyhood? She had dragged him from his studies to go birds' nesting in spring. She had read to him, for hours on end, when he was ill; she who had no knowledge of illness within her own strong body. Many times he had come, creeping along the hedgerows, to seek in her modest home the warmth and love which was absent from the big, formal rooms of the Manor. While her mother sewed patiently before the fire, the two children would play chess, which was the only game in which he showed the greater prowess. In all physical pursuits she revelled in her superiority, bidding silence to the instinct which warned her this must end if one day she were to be more than Richard's friend.

She had no rival for his affection. He had no close friends, save Sir Charles Glynde, amongst the local gentry. He hunted with men of his own class. He talked with the farmers and traders, neither accepted nor rejected by them. He seemed always apart, as she herself was apart, a little suspect because of her standing at the Manor and her learning and the strange, unwomanly trait which made her blood tingle and her eyes shine when the free-traders planned their runs.

Through her cottage window she saw Richard now, handsome in his green coat with the double cape and heavy, silver-buttoned cuffs; the spurs shining on his long black boots, his hair glowing in the sunlight beneath the black cocked hat. The church bell clanged out its summons as he dismounted and tethered his horse to the post beside the lych-gate.

Kate took Judith's arm. "In church you will ask forgiveness for stealing that bunch of ribbons. How you managed it, I know not."

"Oh, it is simple," said Judith proudly. "I know by the silence that nobody is about, and if I were caught with something in my hand, I have but to say I was only feeling it. The gipsies made me practise many times before I was sure I could do it."

"Such things are past, child. You will displease me greatly if I learn that you have stolen, or begged, again."

Judith frowned. "I still do not understand. When you hide these goods from the excisemen, is that not stealing?"

Kate sighed. Patiently she explained it once again, in the way she had learned from Sir Charles.

"It is not stealing, as when you rob someone in the village, or in the market. We, the freetraders, are supplying people with what they desire. We take only from the Government who make unfair laws. If they impose impossible customs duty for brandy and tea and lace and silk, then they must expect to have trouble."

"Yes, I see," Judith murmured, though still she could not follow. But what did it matter? There was but one guiding rule in life now. In the past there had been a succession of people who handed her on, one to another; a confusion of voices, some loud and violent, some quiet but cruel, a few, a very few, right at the beginning of memory, soft and gentle.

Now there was this one presence, warm, dependable; strong arms which held her in her nightmare terrors; a broad shoulder to rest against in those first weeks of delirium; hands which moved gently over her bruised body, a voice blending authority with comfort. After many years—fifteen Kate had guessed—life for Judith was reduced to simplicity at last. She had but to do as Kate told her, and all would be well.

If only she could forget her dreams. The gipsies had filled her mind with strange omens and portents. Sometimes her dreams had come true. But now, for the first time she could remember, she went to church and learned that trying to foresee the future was wrong.

She liked church. She enjoyed the music and the singing—even the sermon which she did not often understand. There was a feeling of peace and security around her. She heard coughing and the shuffling of feet; a child's inquiring voice, a parent's remonstrative whisper. She did not really understand why she should have alternately to stand and kneel and sit; why all these people came to this echoing building which Kate called the House of God.

But obediently she reacted to the pressure of Kate's hand, and offered up her thanks for the happiness she had found for the first time in her troubled life.

The white-haired parson, his joints stiff with rheumatism, climbed slowly to the pulpit. His thin voice trembled as he uttered the words uppermost in the minds of his congregation, expressing their inarticulate thoughts, while their eyes turned incredulously to the Glynde pew, empty and strangely silent. Each Sunday from that pew had issued cheer-

23

ful sounds which set the children giggling and the adults to exchange tolerant smiles. Sir Charles's organ-like notes had reverberated around the ancient walls as, half a verse behind, he joined enthusiastically in the hymns. His rhythmical snores were a familiar, accepted background to the sermon. When he drew out his spotted bandanna handkerchief, the parson would pause in his reading of the lesson, knowing that the ensuing trumpet blast as Sir Charles blew his nose would drown all other sounds for a full minute.

Kate glanced around the church. The men sat stiffly in their Sunday clothes, looking solemn; many women were dabbing at their eyes. With the passing of this genial figure, the village had lost a protector and a friend. His tenants were sure of a fair hearing for their grievances. The children had known that if they skipped after his horse to the end of the village, they would be rewarded by a handful of coins and his gusty laughter as they waved him good-bye. To the women's smiling curtsies he would doff his hat and bow as if they were high-born ladies, and they would pat their hair and smooth down their skirts and repeat for the hundredth time, "There goes a real gentleman."

They filed out of the church now, too absorbed in their shared grief to admonish their chattering children. Kate waited for Richard and walked with him and Judith to the gate. The villagers drew back to let him pass, following with curious eyes the oddly assorted trio.

Beside the churchyard wall, one-legged Jamie leaned on his crutch, his ragged shirt and tattered breeches a target for the scorn of the other children in their Sunday finery.

Kate said, "Sir Charles gave him money, for minding his horse. Perhaps the boy does not know yet—"

She broke off, biting her lip, feeling her eyelids pricking. Richard took out his purse and put a coin into the boy's thin, grubby hand. Jamie muttered some words of thanks and limped down the alley to the ramshackle half-cottage where he lived.

Kate frowned. "That was generous, Richard, but ill-advised. The money will be snatched to fill the tankard of that drunken trollop, his mother. A pair of your discarded breeches, or a coat, would serve Jamie better."

"I will try to remember," he promised, unhitching his horse's reins. "But at present, there are more weighty matters. Tomorrow I shall ride to the Grange to see if there is aught I can do. Still I can scarcely believe it has happened. Yesterday, Sir Charles and I were shooting together, and now—"

She put her hand on his arm. "Shall I come to the Manor this evening? Or do you wish to be alone?"

He smiled into her eyes. "If Judith can spare you for an hour, I shall be grateful for your company."

She watched him as he rode away, a solitary figure on his black mare. On Sundays in the past, he had been accompanied by the bulky, colourful figure of Sir Charles, astride his broad-backed grey. The baronet had relied on Richard to recount the gist of the sermon of which he had heard not a word. In the afternoon, when the parson dined at the Grange, Sir Charles would praise him on the excellence of his delivery and the subtlety of his finer points, and the parson would forgive his host the deception because of the deep humanity shining from the blue eyes regarding him so innocently over a glass of contraband spirits.

Kate sighed as she watched Richard out of sight, and saw the parson walking, with bowed head, to his home.

But by the evening, her spirits had lifted again, as she walked up the long drive to the Manor. A missel-thrush was flinging out an impassioned melody from the topmost branch of an elm. In the damp grass beside the stream, a sweep of wild daffodils gleamed faintly yellow in the fading light. From the lake, hidden by a clump of ilex, came the indignant quacking of a mallard drake. The black mare trotted across the paddock and stretched her neck over the rails. Kate gathered a handful of lush grass from the bank and offered it to this favourite of Richard's horses.

Notwithstanding the peace of the evening, Kate felt again the stirring of a strange unquiet within her. Unable to analyse this new feeling which seemed part of the surge of spring, she tried to put it from her. But it would not be denied, this ache at the heart of pleasure.

The western windows were a dazzle of red in the light from the setting sun, as she emerged from the shadow of the drive. The grey-stoned house, with its mullioned windows and many gables, had mellowed with age and blended now with the soft greens and browns of the surrounding woodland as if it had taken root—forming a harmony of proportion and colour that never ceased to delight Kate.

To Richard, until her coming, his home had appeared as a prison; a series of rooms wherein he ate and slept and did his lessons in a disciplined routine which took no account of the need for love and laughter. He had suffered no physical cruelty. But through the years, a succession of people had done their best to break his spirit. Not a word of encouragement or praise had he received from his governess or tutor. Instead, failure to attend to his studies or produce immediately the required answer, meant long hours locked in the cold, dark schoolroom, or supperless to bed in the vast room reputed to be haunted, where strange sounds filled the night and a branch tapped against the pane with ghostly insistence.

His nerves had become as taut as violin strings. To return to his home after an hour's blissful escape to the lake or the estuary, was like entering a gloomy forest after walking in brilliant sunlight.

It had been left to Kate to point out the beauty that was his heritage and to make him realise that one day he would be master of this gracious house and its estate; no longer a delicate, sensitive boy whose only hope of any peace was to obey.

Kate went to the small door at the side of the house. It had neither the grandeur of the front entrance, nor the servitude of the back. It fitted her status to a nicety, although she did not have any such thoughts as she turned the heavy handle.

When she first came to the Manor, her head had scarcely reached the keyhole and she had clung fast to her mother's hand, a little awed by the size of the house but eager for the adventure of seeing inside. After the first few days, she grew bored. Hour after hour, her mother stitched patiently in the little room set aside for the sewing-woman. They saw only a serving-girl who brought them refreshments, and to Kate's questions she gave no answer save a titter.

"Why do you come here each day, Mama?" Kate asked. "Why can we not stay at home as we did when Papa was with us?"

"Because we must eat, child, and to eat we must have money and for that you must work—unless you are like the people who live in such a house as this."

"Do they not work?"

Her mother lifted shocked eyes. "Indeed no. They are gentry."

Kate shrugged off the problem, though she remembered her mother's words.

One day, bored beyond bearing, her lively mind rebelled against this continued confinement. Creeping behind her mother, softly she opened the door and escaped. She tip-toed along a passage, turned into another, pushed open a door and found herself in the gallery. Beyond, the long beautiful curve of the staircase led her eye downwards, until she saw, through an open doorway, a blaze of logs in a grate bigger than she had imagined possible.

Cautiously she went down the stairs, crouching against the wall. Holding her breath, she peered into the room. In a deep leather chair an auburn-haired boy was reading, lace ruffles falling over his blue velvet sleeve as he rested his chin on a slender, pale hand. Kate's eyes opened wide. She had never seen such a boy as this, dressed in such elegant clothes.

Undaunted, even at seven years old, she advanced into the room. The boy remained absorbed in his book. Kate cleared her throat. The boy looked

28

up, frowning. Dropping his book, he sprang to his feet. He made her a little bow, at which she laughed in sheer delight. Her mother had taught her how to bob when the Squire's coach passed. So now she essayed a curtsy, somewhat unsteadily. Then it was he who laughed, and she though him the most handsome boy in the world.

"Who are you?" he asked.

"My name is Katharine Hardham, but I am called Kate, and my mother is sewing-woman here," she told him in a rush.

"Did the housekeeper send you to me?"

She shook her head, suddenly aware that she was doing wrong. "I must go back. My mother will be cross."

He moved a step towards her, holding out his hand in an odd, appealing gesture.

"No, don't go. Stay and talk to me. I am called Richard—Richard Carryll. I live here, and I do assure you, it is very dull on my own."

"You live here?" she repeated, wide-eyed. "Then —you are gentry, and you do no work."

He laughed again. Then, putting a hand to his mouth, he ran to the door and glanced anxiously around the hall.

"I am supposed to be learning my lessons," he explained. "My tutor will punish me if I do not know the piece he has prepared for me."

"What is a tutor?"

He told her, with a gentle patience which delighted her. The village boys did not talk to her like this. He showed her the book he had been reading. She looked in awe at the shelves lining the panelled room, stacked from floor to ceiling with bound volumes of every size.

"Have you read them all?" she whispered.

Smiling, the boy shook his head. "I think my father has. He spends all his time reading, or studying astronomy. They are the only things he cares for."

"And your mother?"

"She died when I was born."

Shyly she put out her hand and laid it against his cheek. Then she heard voices at the head of the stairs and flew, red-faced, from the library. She took her punishment without a murmur. The thought of the boy was a constant wonder. She was prepared to risk anything to see him again.

Richard, when she left him, put a hand to his cheek where her fingers had rested. Not for years had anyone touched him like that. It was as if a sunbeam had suddenly danced into the room, laid its caress on him, and vanished, filling him with a yearning to recapture its gay warmth.

In spite of obstacles, they found ways to meet. Years of keeping out of trouble and avoiding the grave reproachful presence of his father, had taught Richard means of escape, and secret places where he would not be discovered. For Kate, it was more difficult. Loving her mother, she disobeyed her with reluctance. But her adventurous spirit knew no limits; nor determination any effective curb. And this, she was sure, was not wrong. Richard was lonely. She gave him companionship and lent him the courage of her own fearless nature. She had a great love of learning. Richard passed on to her all his own knowledge, and lent her his books. What could be more natural or more simple?

Her mother accepted the inevitable and welcomed Richard into their modest home, though he came secretly. But when his father died, and he realised that at last he was free of the dominant influence of those who sought to subdue him, the first order he gave was that Kate should come openly to the Manor as his guest and his friend.

She came into the library now, with her quick, firm step, seeming to set the air aquiver with the vitality which flowed into him through her outstretched hands.

"Richard, you are pale. You have been sitting overlong, with naught but sorrow for company, I fear."

She disdained the chair he offered and sank upon the floor, the skirt of her crimson dress spread in soft folds around her. The firelight spread a golden sheen upon her black ringlets.

Sighing, Richard sat down in the leather chair where he had been brooding all afternoon.

"We have all suffered a great loss, but for me— Sir Charles was my only real friend—save for you. He was a man of the world. Yet it mattered not to him that I knew nothing of life beyond this small corner of Sussex, that I had never been to London or taken my place in society."

"But you have not wished to do so."

"You are right. Even so, one day, I must widen my horizons, journey to London at least."

Staring into the fire, she murmured, "Will you take me with you?"

"Of course. You shall accompany me as my sister."

She sat very still, her hands in her lap. She knew he was teasing her. Yet the word "sister" gave her pain. She shrugged off this troublesome sensation, threw back her head, laughing.

"Can you picture me as a lady of fashion? Oh, but I would not disgrace you! I have watched, and listened—when your aunt was staying. See, I will show you!"

Springing to her feet, she ran to the door; then came towards him with mincing steps, her shoulders hunched forward, fluttering her dark lashes.

"La, sir, I do declare I am developing a chill from your plaguey damp weather. I doubt I will survive your coastal vapours. Pray fetch me my warm shawl."

Her imitation of his aunt was so perfect, so ludicrous, that he leaned forward, slapping his knees. He caught her hands, laughing up at her.

"Never change, Kate. When courtesy demanded I should visit their homes, I have had to endure the company of simpering young women. For you to be confined by their codes would be as unnatural as pinioning the wings of the curlew which flies so free over the estuary, or riding always on a bearing rein the thoroughbred straining to go as the wind."

Her voice held a trace of sadness. "But I am not a thoroughbred, Richard. My father was a sea captain, my mother a sewing-woman." She flung up her head. "I am proud of them. My father was brave and honest, his own master; my mother kind and hard-working. Nevertheless, I have not your breeding."

Gently he kissed her hands. "Have I ever taken account of that? I would not have you otherwise, except—"

"Ah! So I exhibit some trait of which you do not approve?"

He stifled the amusement he felt when she used

the formal language of affronted dignity, and retorted gravely, "You know I do not approve of your taking part in a smugglers' run. To dress in lad's clothes now, when you are full-grown to a woman, and to mix with those rough men—"

She wrenched away from him. Her head high, her figure rigid, she exclaimed, "So! You *would* have me pinioned! Think you I can bear life without excitement? That my father's blood does not course through my veins? What adventure is there for a woman, in an isolated village? If I were a man—"

Her shoulders drooped. She held out her hands, so that the firelight playing around fingers and wrist, plainly illumined their delicate structure.

"But I am not a man," she murmured.

He was silent, sensing the clash of temperament within her. With the swift change of mood which still had power to surprise him, she shrugged, smiling.

"So I must do my best with what God gave me. As for smuggling—that I will renounce when the right time comes and not"—she faced him, defiance in her eyes—"not because you tell me."

"Very well," he said mildly. "Since I cannot dissuade you we would be wise to discuss some new plan now that we can no longer use the caves at the Grange."

"For the time being," she added. "Sir Charles has no son. Will not the house fall empty—or perhaps be bought by one of his friends?"

"The property is entailed. Sir Charles has an heir —his brother, Henry—waiting, as Charles once described him, like the bird of prey which is their family device, to seize possession."

"Need that make you look so solemn? You were

Sir Charles's friend and confidant. Surely you can persuade his brother that it will be to his advantage to help us?"

Richard shook his head. "Charles rarely spoke of his brother. They quarrelled so violently that he left instructions that Henry was not to be informed of his death until after the funeral so that he should be spared the hypocrisy of his brother's presence."

"But *you* have no quarrel with him."

"I soon will have, and all others of us who break the law. Sir Henry Glynde is a Justice of the Peace."

She gazed at him with shocked eyes. "Then—everything will be changed! A magistrate almost on top of us! If he is called to take up his duties here, then, the excisemen—"

Chuckling, she broke off. "Oh, Richard, can you imagine their faces? Deprived of their evenings at the Grange when they filled themselves with the brandy they were supposed to be confiscating. I am almost sorry for them."

Richard frowned. "Kate, be serious. This may mean the end of the freetraders in this district."

"Oh, no, never that! A little more dangerous sport, perhaps, where before we have but been playing hide and seek. But we are fifty strong. What can two Preventive officers do against that number?"

"They can appeal for the militia to be called in."

"Poof! We will meet that when it happens."

When he did not answer, she studied his face. "You do not mean—you would give up?" she demanded, incredulously. "You cannot. The men now rely on your judgement, your organisation. For you, there is no need of the money. But for many it is a necessity. The children are well-fed, their clothes are good and warm, their schooling is paid for with contraband money. Would you deny them these comforts?"

He sighed and stood up, leaning his head on the chimney piece.

"You hold me in too high esteem. I assure you, there are others, better fitted than I, to lead the band. There were freetraders working in this district long before I joined them."

"But not so successfully. It was a haphazard affair. Without Sir Charles's money to pay for the bigger cargoes on the other side, without the help of his friends along the route to London—"

He turned swiftly. "There you have it. It was because of Sir Charles, not me."

"I will not have that, Richard. Sir Charles was our backer. But it was you who planned the operations, who rode with his letters, sought out the hiding-places which have proved so safe, allotted each man his special task."

"While there has been no opposition, no danger," he added bitterly. "Do you think I can lead them or control them, if there is to be fighting? Last night—"

"Nobody but I was aware that you—"

"That I was sick with fear?"

She clenched her hands, forcing back the words of scorn she would have used to any other man. After a moment, she rose and put a hand on his arm.

"Think you *I* do not know what fear is? That when you first swam the estuary I did not imagine at every stroke your head disappearing for ever? That when Judith walks out alone, I am not terrified she will fall into some terrible danger?"

"But that is not the same thing. *Your* fears are for others. *Mine* are for myself."

"But you have conquered them, so many times—"

"Only when you are with me."

"Why, then, since I will always be with you, there is no need to plague yourself so."

He turned to face her candid eyes, envying her ability to deal swiftly with a problem or dismiss it from her mind.

"You are my only means of courage, Kate. Without you I should have hidden myself away from life, seeking adventure only in books; riding other men's horses, sailing other men's ships, loving—"

"Shame on you, Richard!" she laughed as he broke off. "Loving other men's wives?"

"No, not that."

"Whom then? Other men's creations, fashioned from printers' ink instead of flesh and blood?"

He stared at her, feeling a strange excitement taking possession of him. Throughout the years, he had regarded her as a dear companion without whom life would have been infinitely lonely. But now . . .

The glow from the fire accentuated the full curve of her breasts above the slim waist. There was a shadowed mystery in the hollow of her neck. Her lips were parted, her cheeks flushed; her dark eyes held a challenge. He saw her in that moment almost as a stranger, as a woman to be desired. Overwhelmed by this revelation, he could neither move nor speak.

Kate took a step towards him, her eyes holding his. With a choked exclamation, he took her in his arms, kissing her mouth, her neck, her closed eyelids. For a moment she remained passive under his caresses. Then her arms went round his neck and with all the ardour of her youth she returned his kisses.

When he put her from him, his action was so gentle she did not realise it was a denial. He turned a little away so that she should not see his face, since she could read his every expression. Bitterly he regretted his impulse. Kate was no light woman to be caressed and forgotten. And he was not ready for anything more binding. He told himself that in love, as in all things, she would demand too much of him. Her giving would be total, her giving and her dominance. He saw himself overwhelmed by her quick passion; reduced, were he to marry her, to an inferior role where his manhood urged him he should be master. Nothing in his long association with this tempestuous girl gave him any inkling that it could be otherwise.

Ashamed of his thoughts, he waited for her to speak. For the first time, he saw her at a loss.

Breathing quickly, her head bowed, she murmured, "I—I must go home. Judith will be anxious."

"Of course." But he did not move.

Tentatively she touched his arm. "You will take me home?"

"Of course," he said again, and turned back to her.

"For the first time in my life," she whispered so low he could scarcely hear, "I wish—but only for your sake—that I had been born a lady."

He said hoarsely, "But you are a lady, Katharine. I would have you none other than as you are." But he knew it was not true, and silently he begged her forgiveness for his deception.

She stood quite still. His words, and the use of

her full name were like a new, delicious taste to be savoured slowly and fully. When she raised her head, Richard's image was blurred by the unfamiliar mist of tears.

"Save when I dress in lad's clothes and join the freetraders," she smiled. "Give me but a little longer, Richard. Do not forbid me yet to stay abed on the nights when the moon is hid."

"*Forbid you?*" he repeated. "When have you ever taken heed of aught I have said? I could as easily forbid the wind to blow as expect you to obey me."

Filled with a momentary sense of disappointment, she failed to detect the note of sadness in his voice. From her bodice she drew out the gold cross he had given her so many years ago. She put it to her lips; then held it out to him.

"Do you remember? How we plighted our troth, so solemnly, amongst the roses that summer evening? See, I have done so again. Now it is your turn."

He stood rigid, his heart racing, his nails digging into his palms, not daring to look at her. He tried to force the words of truth between his tight lips. He felt the dominance of her personality, threatening to overwhelm him. He was free now. He would not be further subdued. It did not occur to him that he was fighting against the very power which had given him strength. He believed that if he weakened now, agreed to marry her, it would mean the destruction of them both. For in his confusion, he believed himself less than her image of him, and in her disillusionment he foresaw the end of love.

The cross gleamed an inch from his mouth. He swallowed hard, seeking desperately for some excuse, however foolish, to save himself from the sacrilege of swearing an oath he had no intention of fulfilling. He raised a trembling hand, pushing the trinket away. For a moment she was puzzled. Then she smiled, a warm, trusting smile which caught at his heart.

"You think I am behaving foolishly?" she murmured. "Perhaps I am. We do not need such vows between us, you and I."

He watched helplessly as she slipped the chain beneath her dress.

"Kate," he began. "Kate—I—" But his voice was only a whisper.

Her eyes were shining, her mouth a full red curve of joy.

"It is late, Richard. Let us walk back along the lane, where all the little sounds of spring will be but an echo of the happiness in my heart."

He went with her down to the village. At her door, he kissed her lightly on the cheek and left her. He walked for hours in the wood. When the dawn spread slowly in the east and he returned to his home, there was but one thought in his head —to escape from the impossible situation into which his own folly had led him.

Fate, next morning, played into his hands. At Falcon Grange, he was handed a letter to be opened after Sir Charles's death, entrusting him with certain transactions in London and instructions to Sir Charles's bankers which would not brook delay. Waiting only to attend his friend's funeral, Richard sent his groom with a written explanation to Kate and set off, with a shamed feeling of relief, on his long journey to the capital.

3

Kate stood beneath the alders beside the stream, dreamily watching the flash of minnows darting amongst the gently moving weed. From a hole in the opposite bank, a water rat poked a cautious nose, flicked its whiskers, and plopped quietly into the water. A trail of bubbles betrayed its passage across the stream. It scrambled on to the mud at Kate's feet, suspiciously eyeing this unfamiliar shape.

A rat discovered scavenging in her larder, would have sent Kate rushing for a stout stick. But now, absorbed in her thoughts, she remained still, fascinated by the delicate tracery of footprints as the creature ran between the tree roots.

The letter from Richard, which had been delivered to her more than a week ago, had, for a space, left a cold, empty feeling inside her. With no word of love to soften the blow, he had stated simply that Sir Charles had entrusted certain matters to him which meant a journey to London at once. How long his stay would be, he did not know—two weeks perhaps. He would bring her a gift, he promised, and news of what really went on in the distant, unfamiliar city.

It was a strange letter, she thought, formal and stilted in tone. But then, she had never received a letter from him before. She shrugged away her disappointment. She knew his inability to make quick decisions, his careful examination of any new idea. And despite that solemn moment in the rose garden eight years ago, the revelation of their love and the prospect of marriage between them had come with as little warning as the first rush of spring through the woods. For her, thereafter, each dawn burst in a thousand flashing sparks of light. For him, she realised, it would mean quiet thought and careful planning for their future together.

But that they should be parted so soon, with no opportunity for a God-speed! She had gone each day to the church to pray for Richard's safety. There were many hazards to be faced; highwaymen and thieves; the roads rendered dangerous by ridges and potholes which could wreck a coach. Sir Charles, expansive after a bottle of port, had entertained them with tales of the city, of footpads and fevers, of the rush of traffic in the evening as the coaches splashed through the mud, and torches flared as the linkboys guided the sedan-chairs.

To her prayers for Richard, Kate added one for herself, since she could not quell a flicker of envy, and the wish that she were already married and so could have accompanied him on this greatest of adventures.

Her thoughts were interrupted by Judith's anxious call. The rat scuttled back into the stream. Kate, shaking herself free from her dreams, returned to the tree trunk where Judith sat, her lap full of primroses.

"I am here. Did you think I had deserted you?"

"It was so quiet. It was like—that other time."

"What other time? Tell me."

She sat on the log, taking Judith's hand. The blind girl's fingers clung to hers, like a child seeking reassurance.

"There is so much I do not remember. But sometimes, in the night, memory comes back." She paused, a shudder passing through her slender body. "I hear a man's voice, loud and angry. I see—for once, long ago, I had sight—I see a woman, arguing with him, and then she is struggling in his arms. He is too strong for her, and she falls and he strikes her with a whip. I remember screaming and the man coming towards me, raising the whip again. And then—then there is nothing but pain and darkness."

Her voice broke. She cowered as if somebody were indeed about to strike her. Kate put a protective arm around Judith's shoulder and held her close.

"Hush, child. It is over now."

When her trembling ceased, Judith asked, "Do you think they were my parents?"

"Who shall say? What more do you remember, of that time?"

"It was in a big house. I remember stables and many horses, and—yes, I went in a carriage and the man, the man with the whip, had silver buckles on his shoes. The lady—who was perhaps my mother—wore a blue dress and—and that is all—" Her voice faltered.

"But that other day—of which you spoke?"

"I do not know how I came to be in the wood. Perhaps that was when I went in the carriage. But I think there was a woman with me and she was crying, and then she went away and I was alone. I walked and walked in the wood. I fell over the tree roots and bumped my head, because by then I was quite blind. I—I was so afraid."

Kate tightened her arm about the girl.

"And then?"

"It is not clear. There were voices and somebody

lifted me. I remember rough hands, taking off my dress and putting on instead something coarse and hard. Somebody gave me food and I think I slept in a hayloft. But I did not understand what they said. I do not know how long I was there, or where I went afterwards, until the gipsies found me."

Kate sighed. There was still no answer to the riddle, despite her coaxing. But perhaps it was best that memory did not return in full. The few details Judith did recall bore out Kate's own conclusion and Richard's, that this waif was of gentle birth. Her face had a delicate beauty; her voice was soft and sweet, her feet had high arched insteps. Under Kate's guidance, she had quickly and willingly abandoned the uncouth language of the gipsies. Who she was nobody knew. She had become a piece of flotsam, tossed from one uncertain resting-place to another, knowing herself unloved and unwanted in a world where only the fit survived.

Starved, beaten and abandoned, she had wandered throughout one cold, wet night, her mind full of strange fantasies. In the bitter dawn, her groping hands had felt walls and windows and cottage door. With a last feeble effort, she tapped on the window. Then, her strength utterly spent, she sank on the doorstep and knew no more.

When she regained consciousness, she found herself in a soft bed, a hot brick at her feet. She felt herself raised up and supported against a woman's shoulder, while a clear, low voice urged her to drink. Afterwards, she lay still, listening dreamily to the quiet sounds as somebody moved around the room, to the crackle of wood as a fire was lit. The fever which was to rage for days, ravaging her frail body, blotting out so much of the past, gave her that one day's respite before its merciless onslaught. In those blissful hours she learned that she was no longer alone; she had but to call out or move uneasily for there to be a voice to comfort, a hand to hold hers in the darkness, and a presence so warm and strong it held all the terrors of her world at bay.

Her long fingers lightly touched the primrose petals.

"I suppose I shall never know—who I am."

"Does it matter so much to you? Is it not enough, that I love you, and will care for you as I would a sister?"

"It is more than enough. But one day, Kate, you will marry, and then—"

"You foolish child! Think you I would not insist that you would stay with me always, that you would come with me to the—"

She broke off. She had kept the happiness of that evening with Richard to herself. When he returned from London, when they were formally betrothed, then she would share her secret. Until then, she held the sweet memory like a candle flame within her, filling her dreams with joy and her future with hope.

She kissed Judith and jumped to her feet.

"Come, this is no time for solemn thoughts. The sun is so warm, the water so sparkling—"

Her eyes filled with excitement. She glanced around to make sure they were alone. Then she kicked off her shoes and white stockings.

"Will you walk in the stream with me, Judith?"

Horrified, the girl drew back. "Indeed, no. It is too cold. Take care you do not drown."

Kate's laughter rang through the trees. "It is not

deep enough for that. Have no fear. I will not go far away."

Hitching her skirt high around her waist, she stepped into the water, a shiver of delight chasing up her spine. She waded to the opposite bank and sat in a patch of sunlight, idly scooping up fine gravel with her toes. Judith's head was bent as she made posies of the primroses.

Suddenly she straightened up, listening.

"Kate, I can hear horses. There is somebody coming."

The older girl strained her ears. But her hearing was not as acute as Judith's. It was a few moments before the sound of hooves reached her.

Where she sat, she was in full view from the bridge. Gathering up her skirts, she started to make her way back. In midstream she stepped on a loose stone. It tipped, flinging her headlong into the water. Gasping and spluttering, she scrambled up, her clothes saturated, her ringlets dripping. Judith jumped to her feet, calling out in alarm. She took a few steps forward, her hands outstretched.

"It is all right," Kate assured her. "I am not hurt, only wet. But— Oh, Lord save us, a carriage!"

Desperately she looked around for cover. "There is a willow here, where I can hide. Do you stay where you are."

The coach, drawn by four black horses, came round the corner of the wood and slowed to walking pace at the approach to the bridge. The coachman, seeing a fork in the rutted road ahead, frowned and shouted over his shoulder to the young footman clinging to the rail behind.

"Which way, do you think? Can you see any sign of a house?"

45

"Not a turret or gable. There is a girl by the stream. Ask her."

The coachman reined in his lathered horses. "Hey, you down there. Which road for Falcon Grange?"

The girl in the simple blue dress did not answer. The man called again, his voice rough with impatience. He wanted to stretch his legs and feel a long drink slide down his dusty throat.

Judith stood irresolute. Uppermost in her mind was Kate's injunction to remain where she was. But the man swore, and now she recognised anger in his tone.

"Have you no tongue in your head, wench? Come here."

In her experience, to disobey such an order could have only one consequence—a hand which sent her stumbling to the ground or a stick laid across her shoulders. She walked forward, uncertainly on the uneven ground.

"What is it you want of me?"

Another voice, younger, gentler, answered. She turned her head to catch the words from the back of the coach.

"We did but hope you could direct us to Falcon Grange."

Judith shook her head. "I do not know the way."

The coachman repeated sarcastically, "You do not know. You live here?"

"Yes. In the village."

"But you do not know the way." He spat contemptuously. "So much for your suggestion, Jonathan. The girl has no wits."

"I doubt that is the misfortune she suffers. I think she cannot see."

The window of the coach slammed down. Kate,

crouched in the willows, saw a man's pale face beneath a black tricorne, the gleaming white of a cravat. The ripple of the stream drowned any words which were spoken. A hand came through the window. She saw the fall of a lace ruffle as a coin was tossed. The money rolled along a ridge of hard earth between the horses' feet.

In Judith a tossed coin provoked an immediate response. Experience had taught her that if she did not instantly retrieve it, somebody with sight would forestall her. She darted downward, ignorant of the danger.

Kate screamed. Starting forward, she tripped. Her sodden dress caught in a tangle of branches, holding her fast.

The coachman swore violently as the rear horses plunged. The footman reached the ground in one wild leap. Recovering his balance, he rushed forward. Grasping the girl, he dragged her back.

To Judith, the world became again a turmoil of threatening sounds—of shouting and screaming, of clattering hooves and the shrill whinny of horses, and then, clear and merciless, a man's laugh.

Distraught, not knowing which way to seek escape, she was imprisoned by strange arms.

"Kate! Kate! Save me!" she implored, her cry a thin wail amidst the confusion of plunging horses.

But it was not Kate's voice which soothed her as the hard arms released their grip.

" 'Tis all over. You're safe now."

She felt something round and hard pressed into her hand. "There, I've picked up the money for you. I'd put you safe on your way if I could. But my master's not a man to brook delay. Stand still while we pass."

47

He folded her fingers gently over the coin. Too dazed even to thank him, she remained quite still as he had told her, and heard the coach rumble on its way across the bridge.

Before the thud of the horses' hooves died away, Kate was beside her.

"You are not hurt? Oh, Judith, I could not get to you!"

The girl said, on a note of wonder, "I thought he was going to take me away. But he was kind, Kate. He was kind and his name, I think, was Jonathan."

"He was more than kind. He was courageous and quick-witted."

"What was he like?"

"A handsome enough lad, I think, though I was not near enough to see his features clearly."

"Of what age?"

"Eighteen years, perhaps. But why these questions?"

The girl's voice trembled. "I felt—suddenly—as safe as I do with you. I never heard a man speak so gently, save Richard." She opened her fingers. "Look. It feels like a florin. He must be rich, the man who tossed that coin."

"Oh, yes, he is rich enough. The coach bore the device of a pair of falcons. Give me that money, Judith."

Kate turned it over in her palm, slowly, deliberately, while anger rose in her like milk to the boil. Then she took the coin between her fingers and thumb and sent it spinning into the stream.

Judith, hearing the plop, raised a horrified face. "Kate! What have you done?"

48

"Thrown Sir Henry Glynde's silver where it belongs, amongst the weeds."

"But it was mine! And—to throw it away—"

"You shall not go without. I will give you as much—more if you wish. I can earn enough for us both, never fear. But think you that I, who have taken wine with Sir Charles Glynde, will accept *charity* from his brother? I, who have helped to fill the cellars of the Grange with brandy—to stand by while the new owner flings a coin beneath his horses' hooves, for *you* to pick up." She broke off, staring with flushed face and dark eyes along the road the coach had taken.

"I heard him laugh," she said between clenched teeth. "I heard him laugh, to see you almost killed."

Ten minutes later, two small boys, astonished to see their schoolteacher with dripping ringlets and a wet mass of clothing impeding her purposeful stride, gleefully called their comrades. But one look from Kate cut short their giggles, and sent them tumbling like frightened puppies, into the nearest alleyway.

Arabella Glynde, weary of the companionship of her father on the two-day journey from London, was provoked into an indiscreet remark.

"That was not kind, Papa."

"To waste a florin on a girl so stupid she could not even tell us the way. You consider that not kind."

"I meant—to throw the coin on the ground. The girl was blind. Could you not have placed it in her hand?"

"And contracted some noxious disease?"

"Oh, no, Papa. She was clean. In fact, she had

49

not the appearance of a cottager's child; she had an air of refinement."

Sir Henry's thin mouth turned downwards.

"Are you unaware that a father often leaves his stamp upon his children? Doubtless my brother has bequeathed many a bastard to this county."

Arabella turned from his contemptuous face. She remembered her Uncle Charles as a big, merry man who dandled her upon his knee and sang rollicking songs whose meaning, fortunately, she was too young to grasp. His gusty laughter had resounded through the quiet London house. The servants, who hovered behind her father's chair like timid, but hostile wraiths, straightened their shoulders and waited upon Sir Charles with deferential smiles. Often she had heard giggles from the young maids, and a scuffle in the passages at night.

Arabella's mother, a frail woman who spent the last two years of her life in bed or reclining on a couch, spoke in scandalised tones of her brother-in-law. Eventually, after frequent quarrels with her father, he came no more; even mention of his name was forbidden. Arabella's questioning of her governess elicited only such ambiguous phrases as "indiscreet behaviour," "criticising the Government," "making your father's position intolerable."

To Arabella's mind, Sir Charles had made life exceedingly tolerable for all around him. His indiscretion, as far as she was concerned, lay in dying before her father, thus abruptly ending the gay life of London society in which she revelled. Already, her father had refused four offers for her hand. At eighteen, her beauty and the knowledge that she attracted the right type of suitor, lent her the self-confidence to indulge the fancy that she would end up no less than a duchess. She found life entirely satisfactory, for even her father's tedious conversation could be endured while she gave half her mind to recalling Mr. Garrick's fine performance or planning an even more fantastic hairstyle for her next ball.

Then, inopportunely, Sir Charles succumbed to his heart attack, and she faced six months' total mourning, and then into nothing but shades of purple or lavender. No balls, no visits to Ranelagh, no supper parties at Vauxhall Gardens under the relaxed chaperonage of her Aunt Maria. She had thought the prospect too awful to contemplate. But worse, much worse, was to follow.

Her father had sent for her one bleak, wet afternoon and informed her they would be setting out for Sussex within the week. She had begged to be allowed to stay in London with her aunt. He had refused her. She had surmised that this visit was for the summer only. He had informed her that henceforth Falcon Grange would be their home. Unbelieving, she had protested.

"But, Papa, I do not wish to be buried in the country. What am I to do in such surroundings? And—more important, where am I to find a suitable husband in Sussex? Have you not read what Mr. Horace Walpole says—that it is a land of Alpine mountains drenched in clouds where the inhabitants are savages?"

"Then it will be my duty to tame them," he replied icily. "As for a husband—I have that in mind. The baronetcy ends with me, but our heritage will go on, through you. Therefore I have no wish for you to marry some foppish young man unworthy of owning an estate such as ours. With your beauty and accomplishments, added to our name, I assure you, there will be no lack of suitors."

For a long moment she stared at the unyielding back he turned to her. Then she burst out, "You are using me as a pawn in your game of petty kingship. My mother was right. All your life you have had this ambition—to inherit the title and the estate, and there to wield absolute power. All those miscarriages she suffered—due to your one desire, to have a son. Now, since you have none, I am to be sacrificed. One would suppose you to be a duke at least, instead of merely a baronet!"

He betrayed his feelings only by the cold glint in his pale eyes and the trembling of his fingers as he took a pinch of snuff. She had been sent from the room, and since there was none other to listen, she had poured out her bitterness into the startled but gratified ears of her maid. In the servants' quarters the details were carefully repeated. In the mind of the new second footman, Jonathan, who had that day been made to run two miles beside the coach in the rain "to test his heart," was piled yet another coal upon the fire of his hatred of Sir Henry Glynde.

A short distance inside the park, Sir Henry left the coach, and walking to the rising ground topped by the beeches, stood looking at the great house he had inherited. He rubbed his hands together in the self-satisfied gesture his daughter found so irritating, while she sat slumped in the corner of the carriage, weary, dusty and dispirited. On his way back to her, he stopped suddenly, staring at the ground. He summoned Jonathan.

"Would you not say that there has been a large number of horses about there recently?"

"Yes, Sir Henry. I should think the hunt stopped here for a space."

"I asked you a question, not for your opinion. There is a trodden path to that chalk cliff. Follow it."

Stiff-faced, Jonathan obeyed the order, his master following thoughtfully. Above the beech hanger they halted, while Sir Henry's narrowed eyes searched the hollow beneath.

"You would surmise," he suggested sarcastically, "that the hunt also halted here, where the fox had gone to earth, since the ground is disturbed around that bramble thicket."

"No, Sir Henry. That's more like a badger's sett."

"Indeed! You consider yourself a knowledgeable young man?"

"I was raised in the country, sir."

"And thereby lack a brain above the farmyard. Go down there and pull aside that bush."

Jonathan stared, hesitating. Then, as he met his master's hard eyes, he scrambled down the bank and, removing his white gloves, pulled at the brambles.

"There is a cavern here," he reported, and disappeared inside. When he emerged, his face expressed disappointment.

"But there is nothing in it, Sir Henry. Did you think to find—?"

"Hold your tongue! It is I who ask the questions, not my servants."

He turned away, and returning to the coach, mused aloud, "I had word there were caves worth investigating at Chichester. But here, upon my doorstep, under my brother's very nose." He halted

53

and once again rubbed his hands together. "Ah, I begin to see."

He took his seat opposite Arabella with a smile on his thin-lipped mouth, but he did not enlighten her as to its cause.

"A few more minutes, and you will enter your new home," he told his daughter with satisfaction.

A brief flicker of curiosity roused her from her apathy. But her first view of Falcon Grange did nothing to raise her spirits. The sprawling, turreted mass of grey stone was in deep shadow, cast by the towering elms and firs. Under the arched doorway the porch looked dark and forbidding.

Arabella stood on the step of the coach, feeling the air strike damp and chill after the sun's warmth through the window. She gazed around her. The green acres of the park stretched on all sides, empty of life save for a group of deer grazing in the distance. There was no other dwelling in sight. Two dogs raced around the corner of the house, their barking a menacing and hostile sound. The raucous quarrelling of many rooks came from the trees above her.

Shivering, she drew back from this prison which threatened to shut out the memory of her London life. Here would be no gay company, no dancing; no walks in the Mall of St. James's or Kensington Gardens; no visits to the playhouse.

Her father, impatient, had already entered the house. Arabella could hold back no longer. She put her hand on the arm outstretched to aid her down the steps and, through misty eyes, read the sympathy expressed in the brown ones of the young footman.

Impulsively, she said, "You were very brave, Jonathan, to save that girl. You might yourself have been kicked."

He smiled as he acknowledged her word of praise. She noticed for the first time how handsome he was, with an unclouded youthful look, his teeth strong and even, his wig carefully curled and powdered.

"She was very pretty, was she not? Though she was little more than a child."

Jonathan blushed, from his neck to his forehead. His voice was husky, and he kept his eyes on the ground.

"Yes, Miss Arabella, she was pretty—pretty as the flowers she dropped. And—and I don't suppose she knows."

Arabella, standing now on a level with the young man, said gently, "Then someone should tell her, Jonathan."

He opened his mouth, closed it again, and swallowed hard. "Sir Henry is calling you, Miss Arabella," he murmured. "It'll be strange for you here at first. If there's aught I can do for you—"

She was pleased by the softness of his voice. In the few weeks he had been in her father's employ she had never heard him say more than "Yes, Sir Henry," or "No, Sir Henry." She supposed it did not even occur to her father that people like Jonathan had any thoughts to express.

She sighed as she obeyed her father's summons. Already the loneliness had started, since she was reduced to exchanging a few words with a servant.

Reluctantly she entered the house. Shivering, despite the fire of huge logs which did little to warm the vast, high-ceilinged hall, she stood gazing up at the face of her uncle beaming down from the portrait above the chimney piece.

"Why did you have to die so soon?" she whispered. "You who professed to love me as a child—how *could* you inflict such a misfortune upon me?"

4

The shock-headed boy, hunched on a stool in a corner of the schoolroom, glanced at Judith, knitting quietly by the window, and winked at the other children.

"There'll be a run tomorrow night, you'll see," he announced.

"How d'you know?"

"The tide and the moon are right."

The innkeeper's spoiled daughter smoothed her skirt and studied her new shoes. "I don't know what you're talking about. What's a run and what has the tide to do with it?"

Her questions were greeted with derisive laughter by the boys.

"A run, you ninny," the tow-haired Willy explained, "is when the brandy and tobacco and silks come in and are hidden away. It has to be at high water for the French ship to come up the estuary, and it has to be dark so's nobody can watch. But *I* watch," he added with a smirk. "I saw it all last time. They came next door—to old Nan Gunter's—with the kegs on their shoulders. Then I heard the horses, much later, going towards the church."

Judith stirred uneasily. "Willy, I don't think you should talk like this."

But Willy was not the boy to be halted by a timid creature like Judith. Besides, there was a row of wide eyes and open mouths confronting him. He lowered his voice.

"I've heard tell they take a girl with them, though she dresses in men's clothes."

"Why should they want a girl?"

"Maybe to bring them luck. Anyway, 'tis little more than women's work now, with the Preventive never seen. In my grandfather's day—"

Judith made another protest. She wished that Kate would come. She could hear her voice outside, telling the crippled boy, Jamie, to stop peering in at the window.

"In my grandfather's day," Willy continued, ignoring the interruption, "there was a lot of fighting. Two Preventive men were killed, just by Farmer Blackmore's. Then the militia came, and some of the smugglers were caught and their bodies hung for weeks in Gibbet Field. My grandfather went to see. He said they were twisting and turning, and the gibbet creaked in the wind, like this—"

He moved his body backward and forward, emitting weird squeaks, his eyes bright with triumph at the effect he produced. Suddenly he saw the changed expression on the faces of his audience. Their heads bent meekly over their books, they shuffled their feet and then were silent.

Willy turned. In the doorway stood Kate, arms crossed, her face impassive.

"That was an excellent performance," she remarked quietly. "Would you like to watch your father—your brother too—swinging like that?"

57

The boy paled and drew back. "No, ma'am."

"Then we must see that you do not cause it to happen." Purposefully she crossed the room. "Your ears hear too much, Willy. We must teach them a lesson."

Soundly she boxed his ears. Yelling, he tried to escape, knocking over the stool. But he was no match for Kate. Seizing him by the collar, she hauled him towards the fire, while the other children clapped their hands to see this know-all knocked off his crowing-perch.

"Do you know what happens to a tongue that says too much?" she demanded. "It has a blazing, hot ember put on it, so that all the words are burned away."

The squeals of delight turned to gasps. The boy hung helpless in her relentless grip, staring at her with enormous eyes.

"Well, boy, what have you to say?"

His bravado gone, his voice came from between blanched lips in a thin quaver. "I—I'm sorry, ma'am. I'll not breathe another word, I swear, about what goes on during the dark nights."

Kate released him so suddenly he fell backwards. She turned to the silent children.

"Now you know, every one of you, what will happen if you speak of these things. Be off with you. But remember this lesson above all others you have learned this day."

They scuttled out, jamming the doorway in their haste to get out of earshot where they could discuss the incident. Kate stood looking after them, her brows drawn together. Then, chuckling, she turned to Judith. The girl crouched against the wall, her hands over her ears.

"Judith, what ails you?"

When the girl did not answer, Kate pulled away her hands and repeated the question.

"You—you would not do it, Kate? You would not really burn his tongue?"

Kate's laugh came from her throat and filled the small room.

"Lord save us, no. It was but a warning."

Judith raised her head. "But you struck him."

"I boxed his ears, the which his mother does every day." She frowned. "Are you taking me to task, Judith? Remember, this is my cottage, my school. I teach the children in my own way; I chastise them as I think fit. I will not be told how I am to conduct my lessons."

Judith sat quite still, all colour drained from her face, while Kate stood above her, hands clenched. Suddenly the blind girl started to tremble, her frail body defenceless against the spasms.

For a moment Kate stared at her, uncomprehending. Then she dropped to her knees and took Judith's hands in her own.

"Child, what is it? Are you unwell?"

Judith made a great effort to control the shudders which racked her. She swallowed hard and, biting her lip, murmured, "There was so much noise. I heard the boy cry out in pain, and your voice raised in anger. I—I was so afraid—"

"Of me? Oh, surely not of me?"

"Of what you would do." She plunged desperately. "Can you not understand, Kate? It sounded just like— All my life there has been shouting and beating and anger. Without sight I could not tell whether the punishment was to be for others, when I would suffer with them, or for myself, when it was

59

already past bearing. But since I have been with you, I have known such peace, such blessed peace."

Kate drew the girl against her shoulder. "And so you shall, child. My poor, poor Judith, forgive me."

She rocked the girl, murmuring words of comfort as she would to a young child. Presently Judith's trembling ceased and she raised her head, smiling tearfully.

"I am being foolish. Of course you must chastise the children and—and me, if I displease you."

"You above all," Kate teased. "From henceforth, I shall beat you every day."

She kissed the girl's wet cheek. "Those days are over, Judith. Nobody will harm you, ever again." She stood up, pulling Judith to her feet. "Come now, it is time we ate." She paused frowning. "I give you warning, though. If those children, or you, repeat one word of what Willy said, one day it may well mean bloodshed where before there has been but a harmless breaking of a most unwelcome law."

As Kate rode down the lane, she heard from under the trees, a horse blowing through its nostrils. She dug her heels into the solid flanks of Tom Blackmore's mare.

Richard came forward to meet her. She hitched the reins over her arm and flung out both hands. Her face, in the half-light under the stars, was alight with eagerness, revealing her heart. All his fine, rehearsed speeches, his resolution, dropped from him. He took her hands, feeling as always the warmth and vitality flowing from her.

"It is so good to have you back," she exclaimed. "I wish that our first meeting could have been where we could talk. There is so much I would ask you —about London, and all you have done and seen. Oh, Richard, I have so many questions. It has seemed so long since you went."

He turned away, feeling the colour flood his cheeks.

"The business I went on kept me longer than I expected."

"So long as it *was* business," she teased. "And you did not lose your heart to one of those simpering misses I have heard you speak of."

The confidence in her voice, the familiar low chuckle, recalling all the happiness she had given him completely disarmed him. From what had he sought to escape? From this woman, whose warmth enveloped him like a cloak, whose strength was for him to share and lean upon? He thought of the vapid creatures he had escorted in London, with their foolish talk and their fluttering eyelashes. He had tried to converse with them as he did with Kate, telling of his crops and his hunting and his books. But it was as if he spoke a foreign language.

There had been only one who held his interest even for a moment—a fair girl who had played the spinet at a large private party. It was the first time he had heard the instrument played with skill and feeling, and it had moved him with a new delight. She had turned as she finished her piece. Across the drawing-room he had met her blue eyes, faintly mocking as she acknowledged the polite murmur of applause. He had bowed gravely to her, hoping to convey his genuine pleasure. She was surrounded by a group of young men, who bore her away. He was too shy even to inquire her name.

He was glad to be home again, back in his familiar surroundings. He had felt out of place in London, and always in his ears Kate's voice had echoed. It was as if she had been there with him, her laughter suddenly throbbing from her throat, to be extinguished by a serious, intelligent question. He had gone away relieved at the chance to escape her. He had returned, as perplexed as he went, knowing only that he was tied to her by some invisible cord, try as he might to break it.

It was evident by the spontaneous warmth of her greeting that never for a moment had she doubted him. Now she waited, expectant but not demanding, leaning slightly towards him, and he could see how her eyes shone, even in the dim light.

He edged his horse closer and bent forward to kiss her on the cheek. But she turned her head so that her mouth was against his, and he felt again the force of the fire he was kindling.

Gently he disengaged himself from her arms. "This is not the time, my Kate. There is much to be done this night. I have not yet told you what I learned today."

She closed her eyes and swayed, as if she were in a dream. Then she shook herself free and gave him her attention.

"This morning I had a message which promises no good to us. It came from Sir Charles's old footman. It would seem that our new Squire is already on the trail. At first light he sent a man riding to Chichester with a note for the Preventive men."

"Richard! But—he can have no inkling. He did but arrive yesterday. Think you one of the servants can have spoken?"

"No. They may serve a new master with their

62

hands; their hearts will remain faithful to the old. I made some inquiries about Sir Henry Glynde in London. It seems he has taken his duties as a magistrate very seriously. Though he will have no jurisdiction here, doubtless he will still consider it his duty to suppress the Trade."

"But—so soon? Do you think the excisemen will come—tonight?"

"If they are summoned, they can do no other than obey." He laughed softly. "They will not find the mist rising from the estuary as warming as the brew Sir Charles prepared for them."

"What will you do?"

"I have it planned. My guess is that there will be only the two local men. Sir Henry would not be so foolish as to ask for an extra force unless he had proof of a run. We will set up an ambush."

"You will not—harm them?"

His horse threw up its head as he jerked at the reins.

"You should know that I would never do that. I joined you only because you persuaded me it was an entertainment more worthy than the chase. If I am to organise the band, there will be no bloodshed. The excisemen will be disarmed, their horses seized, and when it is safe for us, let free."

"Do the men know this?"

"I have already spoken to Jesse. They know what they must do."

Skirting the village, they rode round the inlet. Beyond the dim shapes of ponies and riders merged into the rising mist. Kate experienced once again the pricking of her skin, the exquisite shiver which ran up her spine.

"What task have you for me?"

"Only to stand beside me."

"But, Richard. On such a night as this, each one of us must be of use. Surely there is something of importance that I can do?"

"I have told you—"

"The warning signal! That was what I did before, when we had a zealous coastguard in these parts. I can imitate the redshanks' call so that nobody can tell the difference. Listen—"

She threw back her head and whistled the piping notes. Richard's horse plunged forward. He swore beneath his breath.

"I have already arranged for Silas to give the signal."

"Silas! What does he know of waders' calls? He can but bleat like the sheep he tends all day! You will have all the village turn out to see what strange creature has come upon us if you let him give the warning."

"But Kate—"

"*But Kate. But Kate,*" she mimicked him. "There are no 'buts,' Richard. I shall give the warning. Where were you posting Silas?"

"Beside the oak tree at the corner of the inlet."

"So! A redshank with the voice of a sheep is to call from an oak tree? I' faith, I think London has blunted your wits. I shall hide yonder, in the reeds, and when the excisemen are ten paces past me, then I will call, three times. You will tell Silas to take his horse and load it."

When he did not answer, she said anxiously, "Richard, you understand?"

"Yes. I understand—that you make me look a fool."

"For pity's sake, this is no time for your feelings

to be hurt. You have fifty men's lives in your hands this night. You cannot risk a mistake."

"Fifty men," he repeated. "And two to capture them. You flatter me, Kate. But do as you will. I have no doubt you will prove better than Silas."

At the corner of the inlet he waited while she dismounted. Then, taking the reins of her mount, he left her without another word.

Kate stood beside the seawall, waiting until all the men had gone past. Jesse Turner, the innkeeper, leaned from his saddle.

"What did you do to my Betsy, Mistress Kate? She came home nigh scared out o' her wits."

" 'Tis better for her to be scared than clacking her tongue over Willy's tales. I did but box his ears to close his mouth."

"So that was it? If he were my boy, I'd tie him up o' nights. His eyes are like hawks' and he's slippery as an eel. You'd best speak to his father."

"There is no need. I think he will not talk so wildly again."

" 'Tis to be hoped not. If Sir Henry Glynde is sniffing out the ground, we want blank faces in the village and not children's thoughtless chatter. You're to give the warning?"

"Yes."

The big man heaved himself upright. "Good. Your eyes and ears are sharper than Silas's. You've brought us much good luck, Mistress Kate. 'Twas a hard blow when Sir Charles died, but Mr. Carryll has planned our new hiding-places well. There's little can go wrong."

"You are not afraid, Jesse?"

He guffawed; then clapped a hand over his mouth.

"Afraid? Of those two chicken-hearted runts from Chichester? I'll dangle them one from either hand."

"I meant—that Sir Henry Glynde is a Justice of the Peace?"

Jesse spat contemptuously. "I saw him pass in his coach yesterday. A man with a face like a tallow candle and eyes so pale it seemed they saw no more than poor Judith's."

"He has the law behind him."

"What of that? The law is no use to him unless he catches us, and he'll not do that."

"The Preventive men will, if you stay talking here," she laughed.

She heard him chuckle as he urged his horse forward. She felt a great warmth towards Jesse. He had led the band until she had persuaded Richard to join them. Then, recognising Richard's superior brain, the advantage they would gain from the patronage of Sir Charles Glynde, Jesse had surrendered his place to Richard with generous good nature. It was a pity he spoiled that daughter of his so outrageously. She had learned not a thing at her lessons, caring only for the silver buckles on her shoes, or a new ribbon for her bonnet.

Kate found a hiding-place amongst the reeds, revelling in the freedom of movement afforded by breeches. Yet—perhaps there would be a bale of silk in the Frenchman's cargo.

She would make herself a new dress, ready for Richard's coming of age, so that he would be proud of her.

She raised her head, listening intently. The sound of horses' hooves came faintly from the village. It seemed an eternity before the riders came into view, silhouetted against the sky. She began to count when they drew level with her.

Then, across the inlet, the notes of a startled red-shank rang out, three times. She heard the stifled exclamation of the excisemen as their horses shied. Then silence. Beyond, in the oak grove, a light appeared. The two riders whispered together. She heard the creak of saddles as they dismounted.

She longed to vault over the sea wall and run to where the ambush would take place. She clenched her hands and bit her lip, her heart beating wildly. With all her mind she willed the two men to answer the lure. She could see nothing but the glimmer of the lantern, flickering between the trees. Then it was lost to sight. Straining her ears, she waited, while the sea lapped gently over the mud.

There was the crack of breaking branches, a shout. Then muffled grunts. Then silence.

It took all her will-power to remain at her post. But there might be reinforcements. She must stay, listening and watching.

After what seemed too long an interval, she saw three flashes of light from the grove. She turned towards the estuary. Across the still water an answering light betrayed the presence of the lugger.

Kate let out a long sigh of relief. So it had gone well. She settled down to wait, eyes and ears alert.

The Frenchman's light went out. She heard the familiar sounds as the file of men and ponies came around the inlet—the jingle of harness, the muffled thud of hooves, a stifled oath as a horse stumbled on the rough ground. When the long line had passed, she stood up, easing her cramped limbs.

She walked to the grove of oaks, and found Richard.

Without speaking, she put her hand through his arm. On the ground a few feet away lay the two excisemen, trussed like chickens.

Jesse's deep voice was amused. "You did well, Mistress Kate. I could scarce believe 'twas not a real bird."

"It went smoothly?"

He pointed a thick finger. "You can see. I've been trying to persuade Mr. Carryll to leave them as a gift upon Sir Henry's doorstep."

"I told you not to use my name," Richard muttered.

Kate pulled on his arm. "But what a splendid idea! We used to leave Sir Charles his brandy. Why should not his brother have a present also?"

She suppressed a chuckle as she felt Richard's restraining hand on hers.

"If you wish to put your head in a noose, I have no desire to follow suit. These men will remain here until dawn. Then we shall release them and they will ride to the Grange and report that they saw and heard nothing untoward. You have convinced them that is what they must do, Jesse?"

"Ay, they'll do as they're bid."

"How can you be sure?" Kate whispered.

Jesse's smothered guffaw was like wind roaring through the trees. "In the same way as you made sure of that boy's idle tongue. They have no more a man's spine than young Willy."

The file of men had gone on their way, winding through the valleys beneath the silent Downs, thrusting through the secret tangled lanes. The shapes of riders and baggage, above the mist which enshrouded the horses' legs, appeared like ghostly galleons moving steadfastly through the night. There had been a big landing. Some of the cargo had been stowed in Nan Gunter's cottage, in the cellars of the inn, the hollow tombs in the churchyard.

Kate, astride Tom Blackmore's mare, rode with Richard and twenty men to the new hiding-place, the downland caves near Chichester. It had been as easy as a child's game of tag, she thought. Yet Richard seemed withdrawn. Even on the return journey, when there was nothing to betray their night's work save a few kegs they kept back as presents, she could sense his tension.

They halted by the lane to Tom Blackmore's. The band split up, the men making their way home to their farms or isolated cottages or down through the shadowed alleys of the village.

Kate said lightly, "A good night's work, Richard. Everything went smoothly."

"Yes. This time."

"Is that not enough? What we have done once, we can do again."

"I am not so sure. I have already left my card at the Grange. I shall call on Sir Henry Glynde tomorrow, though it may seem a little soon."

The laughter rose in her throat. "Oh, Richard, to think of you, drinking his wine, making polite conversation, listening to how the excisemen failed to catch a single freetrader. I' faith, I would dearly love to be there."

His black mood dropped from him. It had been present ever since Kate insisted on giving the warning. He knew she had completely forgotten their argument; that it was foolish to resent her high-handedness. Tomorrow's visit to the Grange, which he had been dreading, when he would have to assume a show of ignorance, suddenly appeared to him in a different light.

"I wish it too, Kate. But I will relate it all to you. 'Tis said he is a man who does not laugh—"

"Does he not?" Her voice was low and fierce. "You are mistaken. He can laugh—oh, yes, there is no doubt of that. But his laughter is of the devil—without pity."

"Kate! What is this strange talk?"

She relaxed and stretched out her hand.

"It is nothing that need trouble you, Richard. The hurts that are done to Judith do not call to you for redress."

"You take too much upon your shoulders."

She shrugged. "They are broad enough. Broader, I wager than many you saw in London."

For a brief moment he recalled the shoulders of the girl who had played the spinet, shapely and white in the blaze of candles. He imagined how they would feel beneath his fingers, so cool and soft. He closed his eyes, trying to shut out the impossible memory. He felt Kate's hand against his cheek.

"You are weary, Richard. And the mare droops beneath my weight."

"And you?"

"Oh, I am rarely tired. But now my bed appears welcome, if Judith will sleep quietly and let me stay in it."

"She still has nightmares?"

"Not every night. Often now she is at peace the whole night through. And then—oh, then, she wakes like a child in the morning, with such eagerness for the day." She paused, and then added softly, "As I woke this morning, knowing you had re-

70

turned to me. I thought the birds had never sung so sweetly, nor the sun bade me such a bright good morning. I wanted to run and skip like the children and cry aloud that in a few hours I would see you, hear your voice, touch your hand. Oh, Richard, my love—"

He caught her to him. But his hands, holding her, felt only the coarse cloth of her man's jacket, concealing the soft warmth of her body. She snatched the kerchief from her head. She took off his tricorne and drew down his head to lie in the curve of her neck while her loosed hair fell around him. She held him, straining her arms about him, until a movement of his horse forced them apart.

She uttered a long, shuddering sigh. "Good night, my own dear love," she murmured. "I will come to you tomorrow evening, to hear all your news."

He kissed her hands as he took his hat, and murmured a farewell. It was not until she had stabled the mare, leaving a keg of spirits hidden under the hay, that she realised they were the only words Richard had spoken. But what need was there of words? Had he not held her and kissed her, and given himself up to the circle of her arms?

She walked with her long stride, unimpeded by skirts, down to the village, past the church, to her cottage. At the door, hearing footsteps, she turned to whisper a good-night to the blacksmith. Then, with a sigh of contentment, she entered her home.

From behind the tombstone just inside the churchyard, a boy's figure emerged. As he crept, barefooted, to his home, the unrepentant Willy gave a satisfied yawn and considered his sleepless night well spent.

5

Richard woke late next morning. He stretched and turned over, thumping his pillow in an unconscious protest against the onset of day, and tried to escape once more into sleep. But it was as if Kate were in the room, rousing him, stirring him to reluctant action. Muttering, he pulled the bedclothes over his head.

He remembered how last night she had hurried forward, hands outstretched, to welcome him. He felt as helpless as the sea, pulled this way and that by the moon. But Kate was not like the moon, pale and cold and remote. The sun was her image. And if the sun should burn white-hot, should he not rejoice and be grateful, rather than seek the solitary shade?

He rang for his valet, jerking at the bell rope. He dressed in the fawn buckskin breeches, mulberry coat and sprigged gold waistcoat he had bought in London, and went down to breakfast. The house seemed dark. Outside, a sea-fret almost blotted out the garden. Relieved, he gave up his project of visiting the Grange and ordered a fire to be lit in the library.

But after half-an-hour's attempt to concentrate on a book, he gave it up and wandered aimlessly round the shelves, picking out a volume at random, glancing at it with unseeing eyes.

Had all gone well last night? Had the Preventive men kept their oath of silence, and reported all quiet to Sir Henry Glynde? He should have gone back, and not relied upon Jesse. Yet it was Jesse's deep boom which could best hold a threat. His own voice could be too easily recognised. He recalled with a twinge of anxiety how the innkeeper had addressed him by name, in that gusty whisper as loud as many a man's normal voice.

He started violently as a log fell in the hearth. His hands felt cold. He held them towards the blaze; but he felt no warmth.

Suddenly, desperately, he wanted Kate, wanted to lay his head on her shoulder as he had last night, with her dark cloud of hair shutting out the world. He turned and strode across the room, his one thought to go to her. At the door he paused, his shoulders slumped. She would be in the middle of lessons, surrounded by children. Somehow his day must be filled, the hours passed, until she was free to come to him. She would come, through this same door, her cheeks glowing, her hair curling with the mist, and she would say . . .

He knew, only too well, what she would say. "You did not ride to the Grange—because of a sea-fret—when your mare knows every inch of the way! Oh, Richard, for shame!"

He wrenched open the door and shouted for his mare to be saddled. He flung himself into his riding-coat, snatched up his tricorne and strode outside. Flicking with his whip at the mounting-block, he waited impatiently until two dark shapes emerged from the mist. He saw the startled face of his groom as earth and stones spurted from the rearing hooves. He rode down the drive as if bent on breaking his neck.

A great fire of beech logs burned in the hall of

Falcon Grange. But the man who stood before it, hands clasped behind his back, seemed made of ice. Above him, Sir Charles, his ample figure arrayed in rainbow hues and surrounded by adoring dogs, seemed by contrast to be so alive it was as if he spoke from the canvas: "All in black for me, Henry. That is hypocrisy indeed!"

Reluctantly, Richard lowered his eyes from the portrait and stepped forward. His ears, remembering the genial voice of the Grange's former owner, were offended by the lifeless, precise tone of Henry Glynde.

"You are prompt in your call, Mr. Carryll. May I attribute this to neighbourliness, or curiosity?"

Flushing, Richard answered levelly, "I had the honour to be your brother's friend, sir."

"And you hope to be mine?"

Abashed by the coldness of Sir Henry's tone, Richard bowed before he took the chair the baronet indicated by a small gesture of his thin, white hand.

"I do not make friends, Mr. Carryll, only acquaintances. Friendship lessens a man's power, since thereby he may find his affection and his duty at odds."

"And to you, sir, I surmise duty is everything?"

Sir Henry pulled back his shoulders and swung on to his heels.

"Just so. I intend to pursue it—against all obstacles."

Since the older man was regarding him fixedly with pale, expressionless eyes, Richard asked, "You —you have some particular duty in mind, sir?"

"Indeed I have. The suppression of smuggling activities in this neighbourhood."

74

Richard, studying his mud-flecked boot, inquired casually, "You have reason to believe—?"

"Every reason." He took out his silver snuffbox, hesitated, then replaced it in his pocket as if he could not allow himself even that indulgence. "Since you frequently visited my brother, sir, you are doubtless aware that his stock of brandy appeared —unlimited?"

"Sir Charles was ever a generous host."

"It would appear that his generosity outran his prudence."

Richard looked up quickly. But the older man, his thin brows drawn together, was staring out of the window.

That is something you need not fear, Richard thought. The baronet's angular body, the narrow forehead beneath the old-fashioned wig, his sharp-ridged nose and bleak mouth—were the absolute negation of generosity.

The grandfather clock ticked on in the vast hall, emphasising the silence. Richard cleared his throat. His host glanced round as if he had forgotten the other's presence.

"You have lived at the Manor a good many years, Mr. Carryll?"

"All my life."

"Then you are doubtless aware of what goes on in this neighbourhood?"

"Not altogether. I—I am something of a recluse and have never taken much part in the social life —not that there is a great deal. We are a small community in this corner of Sussex."

Embarrassed by the other's stare, he broke off.

"I was not referring to the social life, but to the activities which I have already mentioned."

"I believe there was some traffic in contraband goods some time ago."

Sir Henry pursed his lips. "Some time ago. That is all you are prepared to say?"

Richard jumped to his feet. Suddenly losing patience with this inquisition, it was as if he heard Kate laughing beside him, urging him to recklessness.

"What would you have me say, sir? That there are kegs of brandy hidden in every nook and cranny of my house, and I am the leader of these outlaws?"

A soft, rippling laugh sounded from behind him. Richard swung round. His hands fell to his sides, while he stared, open-mouthed. For a moment he could not collect his senses.

Halfway down the stairs, elegant in a full-skirted black silk dress with long lace ruffles falling over her elbows, stood the girl he had seen but once and remembered so vividly. Her shapely shoulders were hidden now by a drapery of white lawn, and a little cap covered all but the ringlets of her fair hair. But in her blue eyes was the same slightly mocking smile with which she had regarded him across the crowded salon.

As from a great distance, he heard the baronet's voice.

"Allow me to present my daughter, Arabella, sir."

She moved slowly down the stairs, her hand extended in a graceful, languid gesture. Rising from his bow, he saw that she was studying him with interest. He was thankful to have donned his new clothes for the visit. He wondered if his unpowdered hair would dub him as a simple countryman in her eyes.

With smooth, gliding steps, she crossed to the bell-rope.

"You will take a cup of chocolate with us, sir? Although your words made it seem more fitting we should bar the house against you and arm our servants."

Her soft laughter rippled out again, accentuating her dimples. She sank into a chair and laid her hands demurely in her lap. She looked up at Richard, her eyes mischievous.

"Do you haul the barrels up the cliffs on pitch-black nights, Mr. Carryll? Pray tell me, is that how 'tis done?"

"We have no cliffs in West Sussex, madam."

"No? Then, what is the procedure?"

Richard glanced at her father. But Sir Henry's attention was on the door and his face registered disapproval of the tardiness of his servant's appearance. Richard bent over Arabella's chair and answered softly, "We tie the casks to our horses' tails and drag them in that fashion all the way to London."

Delighted, she smiled at him. Perhaps life in this outlandish corner of England was not to be so intolerable. Intending to ride through the park to the village that morning, she had been confronted on rising, with a damp greyness swirling past her window. She had resigned herself to a session with the housekeeper when she saw the groom walking a strange horse in the yard. Anxious not to miss the chance of any distraction, she had changed her dress and come downstairs.

It was Jonathan who incurred Sir Henry's displeasure when he eventually appeared with a silver tray. But Richard was not to escape censure.

"I would not recommend you to talk idly of these matters in the presence of a former magistrate, sir. I am not naturally given to appreciating jokes of such a nature."

Richard, sipping his chocolate, felt his colour rising. Arabella, ignoring her father's rebuke, inquired lightly, "You are no doubt acquainted by sight with many of the village people, Mr. Carryll? Is it possible you have some knowledge of a blind girl of—oh, some fifteen years?"

Richard noticed that the young footman hesitated, then moved a table an unnecessary inch nearer Arabella.

"That would be Judith."

"Judith. A pleasing name. She lives, perhaps, in the little cottage beside the wood?"

"The gamekeeper's cottage? Ah, no, Judith lives with—with Miss Hardham, who has the dame's school in the village."

Arabella glanced at the footman, hovering beside her chair. "That will be all, Jonathan," she murmured, and was amused by the devotion in his eyes as he bowed himself out.

She turned her attention again to Richard. "If you are not truly a smuggler, sir, how do you occupy your time in this damp, cold county?" She gave an exaggerated shiver, holding out a shapely hand to the fire.

"There are the pursuits of the country, madam —shooting, fishing, the chase. Also, I read a great deal."

She arched her delicate brows. "Do you not give balls, or private parties? Oh, in London now, there would be so many delightful entertainments."

She clasped her hands together, her eyes shining,

and leaned forward in her eagerness. Sir Henry put down his saucer with a clatter.

"You appear to forget, Arabella, that you are in mourning."

She sat stiffly upright and laid her hands on her black skirt. With bent head, she murmured, "You are right to remind me, Papa. I am sorry. It is difficult to realise that my Uncle Charles is no longer alive."

There was a catch in her voice. Richard stretched out an impulsive hand towards her.

"I share your sentiment, madam. He was so good a friend to me. Many times he gave me sound advice regarding the management of my estate."

"You are without a father?" she inquired softly.

"And mother too. She died when I was born."

"I am sorry."

His hand lay on the arm of her chair. For a brief moment she rested her fingertips lightly on his wrist. It was as if a butterfly had touched him, sending a shiver of delight up his spine.

Her father had moved to the window. "The mist has almost cleared," he announced. "You will have no difficulty in finding your way home, Mr. Carryll."

Arabella caught her lower lip between her teeth. The delicate colour crept up her neck. She gave Richard an appealing, helpless look, as embarrassed by so obvious a dismissal, he rose to make his adieu. Arabella's smile was no longer faintly mocking. It held, he thought, a hint of sadness. As, with drooping shoulders, and no colour—not even a hint of paint on her face—to relieve the total sobriety of her appearance, she bade him good-bye, she looked very small and lonely in the sprawling, solid mass of Falcon Grange. Her image so filled his mind that it was with a start of surprise he found his mare, slack-reined, had carried him safely home.

He sat down to dinner unmindful of what was placed before him. Afterwards he wandered into the drawing-room, so little used it felt as cold as a cave. He crossed to the spinet from which no note had sounded since his mother's death. For a long time he stood staring at the instrument like a man bewitched.

Kate twirled her glass so that the candle-light, shining through the wine, threw off a golden glow.

"I would that I could paint," she sighed.

"But you can," Richard argued mildly.

"Paint properly, I mean—like an artist. So that I could transmit to canvas the sparkle of this glass, the glint of the silver facings against the purple velvet of your coat, the firelight shining on your hair, making it the colour of—oh, of a copper warming-pan. You look so handsome this evening, Richard, in your new London clothes."

He moved uneasily in his chair. But Kate, sipping her wine, went gaily on.

"There was a roll of green silk in Nan Gunter's cellar. It is too fine a stuff for a schoolma'am. But it would do well for—for when I am married. With the help of the fashion journals you brought me from London I shall make it up in the latest style."

His fingers closed round the stem of his wineglass so hard it all but snapped.

"But green, Kate? I thought—with your superstitions—"

Dismayed, she exclaimed, "Oh, I had not thought! I must choose again. I would not risk bad luck—

not now, when living has become so joyous an adventure."

He forced himself to look at her. She sat forward in her chair, her eyes shining, her whole body held in leash against the desire to go to him. He remembered, as if the experience were not his own, the yearning he had felt for her that morning. Now he had but to hold out his arms and she would cross the space between them and once more envelop him in the warm passion of her love.

But he could not make that move. Was it to be ever thus? That when she was away from him, he longed for her, feeling a part of himself to be missing, yet in her presence, to be afraid of her strength, struggling like a drowning man against the wave which would engulf him?

She uttered a little sigh and sat back in her chair.

"But there are more important matters to discuss than the colour of a new dress. Come, tell me, you had speech with Sir Henry Glynde?"

He crossed his legs, smoothing an imaginary wrinkle from one white stocking, studying the silver buckles on his shoes.

"Yes," he said at length. "It seems impossible that those two were brothers. He is a frigid man, without humour. He appeared to be suspicious of my activities."

"But that is nonsense! There is nothing—no clue at all—to connect you with the freetraders. We have never hidden any contraband in your house; you use a horse that is never seen outside your grounds in the daytime; you forbid the men to use your name. How is it possible for him to suspect you?"

"Because I was Charles's friend, I assume."

"He *knows*—about his brother?"

"I am not sure. He is a man who does not change his expression or his tone of voice. You cannot tell what he is thinking."

"Did he not even appear put out that the Preventive officers reported they had seen nothing—for I surmise they did so report since all is quiet."

"I do not know. He did not mention—"

"But, Richard, that is what we all wished to learn. It is why you went so soon to call upon him. I' faith, London *has* dimmed your wits!"

Concerned only with evading her scorn, he explained, "It—it was not possible. We had spoken for only a short while when his daughter joined us."

He heard Kate's indrawn breath, and though he avoided looking at her, he sensed the stiffening of her whole body.

"So! Sir Henry has a daughter? You did not tell me this before."

"It seemed of no importance."

"*Seemed!* And now—?"

He rose and poured her out more wine. Her eyes were on his hand. Annoyed, he saw it was not altogether steady.

"Of what age is this daughter? A child, or—?"

"I would surmise—about your own age."

"And she has just come from London. She was dressed fashionably?"

Impatiently, he gulped his wine. "How should I know? She is of course in mourning."

"Beautiful?"

"I—I think she would be considered so."

"By you?"

"Why, yes, Kate. She has elegance, and—and a kind of delicacy, as Judith has—"

She drained her glass and slammed it down so

that it fell off the table, and broke upon the floor.

"And I have not! Is that what you are thinking, Richard?"

Helplessly, he faced her blazing eyes, searching for words to mollify her. Suddenly she put her hands to her face, hunched her shoulders and turned from him. Horrified, completely at a loss, he saw that she was weeping.

Somewhere, sometime, he knew he had seen her act like this. Desperately he stirred the embers of memory. An image formed in his mind, an image of Kate coming to him one winter's day, not speaking, but simply burying her face against his shoulder. He had held her, not knowing the cause of her distress, until at last she had told him in a strangled whisper that her mother was dead.

She had been little more than a child then. Blind instinct told him this was the same reaction, that for some reason he could not fathom, she was hurt.

Praying he was doing the right thing, he knelt and took her gently in his arms. For a moment she held herself stiff, resisting him. Then she relaxed and laid her cheek against his hair.

"Forgive me, Richard. I am as foolish as all other women, after all. Only I could not bear to lose you. I—I love you so."

He tightened his arms about her and kissed her fingers.

"Why should you lose me?"

Her voice was low. It held a note of humility he had never heard before.

"I know full well that if—if you moved in society, as you should; if you stayed long in London, met young ladies of fashion, you would not wish for my company."

"That is nonsense," he told her gently.

"No. It is the truth. My father was a sea captain, my mother a sewing woman in your house. Those were my origins. What I have become since, Richard, you have made me."

"Then I am proud." He looked up at her, smiling. "And since *you* have so persistently moulded *my* life, we are bound to each other."

She caressed his cheek, smoothed back his hair. "Those are the words I have been waiting for you to speak—ever since that first night—those, and three others."

"What others?"

The thick lashes hid her eyes as she answered. "That you love me."

"Then I will say them now. I love you, Kate. There, now are you happy?"

He felt the movement of her body as she gave a deep, contented sigh. She held his head against her breast and was quite still, her eyes shadowed and dreamy.

"If only," he began, then stopped himself. It did not seem wise at that moment to say, "If only you could always be like this, my Kate."

6

Kate and Judith came down from the woods, their baskets full of bluebells. In Judith's cheeks was the pink flush of restored health; the dark hollows beneath her eyes had disappeared. She held her head on one side, like an inquisitive bird, listening to everything that went on around her. She could name each child now; she had learned to move easily about the cottage and how many steps would take her from one village shop to another. This morning, carefully feeling each trinket put into her hand, she had selected a brooch for Kate. Proudly she bore it home, the first present she had ever bought, with the money she earned from basket weaving. Kate had assured her it would be her most treasured possession, save only the gold cross Richard had given her so many years ago.

Beyond the village, the placid waters of the estuary glinted in the sunlight. A fishing boat put off from the quay, disturbing a heron which rose from the reeds and flapped ponderously over the mudbank. Kate, following its flight, was describing it to Judith when she stopped in mid-sentence.

Beside the church stood a groom with two horses, one bearing a side-saddle. Judith, immediately sensitive to every change in Kate, asked anxiously, "Why did you stop? What have you seen?"

"I am not sure. But I think—"

Kate's eyes narrowed. She hurried Judith forward and bade her wait beside the lych-gate. She walked quietly along the path between the gravestones and slipped into the shadow of a buttress.

A young woman in an elegant black riding-habit was walking slowly beside the sea wall, bending to read the inscriptions on the stones. Or pretending to read? Kate watched, her brows drawn together. In another moment, the girl would be close to the hollow tombs where a quantity of kegs lay snugly buried. For those with observant eyes, there might well be tell-tale signs, footprints on the earth, a scattering of moss, even a sliver of wood ripped from a barrel. Was this the new Squire's next move —to send his daughter innocently to search for clues? For Kate had no doubt of the stranger's identity.

She moved out of the shadows as Arabella reached the hollow tombs. She gave her a perfunctory bow.

"I can procure you a key, ma'am, if you wish to enter the church."

Startled, Arabella looked up. She saw a handsome girl whose dark eyes held hostility, despite the courtesy of her words.

"It is kind of you. But—another time, perhaps. I must return now."

Kate's brows rose in an unspoken question. Arabella, unused to such a level, distrustful gaze, found herself explaining as if she had committed a trespass. "I did but come to visit my uncle's grave—"

"But Sir Charles is buried near the gate, Miss Glynde. You could not fail to see—the new headstone, the flowers."

"I—I have already added mine. I thought to—"

Suddenly realising she was acting like a guilty child before this bold and forward girl, Arabella looped her skirt over her arm and stepped on to the path. She inclined her head in the slightest of acknowledgements and passed on, with her smooth, gliding walk.

She paused at sight of Judith, waiting patiently beside the low wall. To Arabella, a blind girl with a muddied skirt, standing outside a church gate holding forward a basket of flowers, had only one significance. She took her net purse from a pocket of her habit.

"Your flowers are so pretty," she remarked. "And they smell so sweetly."

Judith, reacting instinctively to such a voice, to the sound of jingling coins, held out the bluebells in one hand, while her other lay open, palm upwards. Her voice slid automatically into the whine taught her by the gipsies.

"They are fresh, lady, only picked an hour ago."

Arabella accepted the flowers and was proffering the coin when it seemed the furies of hell invaded the churchyard and bore down on her in a blaze of crimson.

Kate caught Judith's outstretched hand, holding it fast within her own. She faced Arabella, her shoulders flung back, her head high.

"You are welcome to the flowers, ma'am. But we take no payment for what nature provides so lavishly."

Arabella's face was as white as the cravat round her slender throat.

"I was not aware that you were concerned in this," she said icily. "I offered the money to this poor girl."

"What you offer to Judith, you offer to me."

"She is—your sister?"

"In all but name."

"Then you should not frighten her so. See, she is terrified by your anger."

Kate's voice was low and husky. "You dare to tell me how I am to treat Judith! You—the daughter of the man who all but killed her with a coin tossed so carelessly beneath his horses' hooves. Were you also in the carriage? And did *you* join in his laughter?"

Arabella stepped back, appalled at the bitterness

87

in Kate's voice. For a moment she thought this broad-shouldered girl was about to strike her. Instinctively she raised her whip.

Suddenly she was aware of an unnatural silence, of her groom's anxious face as he walked the horses towards the gate. She looked around her.

In every doorway stood the women, some with toddlers at their skirts. Topping the churchyard wall was a row of children's faces, wide-eyed, fingers in mouths. She realised that this was not mere idle curiosity. Under the silent watching she sensed their animosity towards herself. The reason she did not understand. She had encountered nothing like this in London, and was at a loss to deal with such veiled hostility. She could only suppose they were enjoying the spectacle of herself, a stranger, being bettered by this virago who was one of themselves.

The groom, waiting with downcast eyes, was her only link with the complacent smoothness of her sheltered life. But she noticed that he did not raise his eyes as he aided her to mount. Her nerves already stretched by her hatred of the cold, masculine atmosphere of the Grange, she could not bear the uncanny silence any longer.

Erect in her saddle, she turned to Kate.

"I apprehend you are Miss Hardham. It is a pity you do not teach your pupils better manners than you have yourself."

She wheeled her horse and rode down the village street. Though she looked neither to right nor left, she was acutely conscious of the women, bobbing curtsies to her, with not a twitch of the tight muscles which pulled their faces into blank, but oddly triumphant masks.

Kate stared after her. Then, reassuring Judith,

she stooped to retrieve the scattered bluebells. Ashamed of her outburst, she sought to justify it. But, try as she might, she could not hide from herself the true cause of her animosity towards Arabella. Richard's words hammered in her mind: "She has elegance and a kind of delicacy."

She knew them to be justified, and with the knowledge came the first tiny quiver of doubt. On what were her dreams founded? On a childhood promise, on a few words of love extracted from Richard under pressure of tears. There had been no proposal, no mention of marriage on his part.

Over their heads as she and Judith had emerged from the woods had flown a black and white, chatering bird. A single magpie. "One for sorrow . . ."

Richard stood at the drawing-room window, smoothing the lace ruffles beneath the heavy cuffs of his purple coat. In the garden, the torturing wind was breaking the spines of the spring flowers, scattering vivid petals on the wet earth. A scurry of leaves danced wildly across the lawn; the rooks cawed a loud but futile protest as their nests swayed dangerously in the elms, threatening to tip out their offspring. The rain, sweeping up from the southwest and trailing its grey cloak across the estuary, beat a staccato fusillade against the windows.

Richard turned, frowning, as smoke billowed from the wide chimney. He glanced round the room, trying to see it as a stranger would. Nothing had been changed in the house since the death of his mother, twenty years ago. So infrequently did he entertain that for months the drawing-room furniture was enshrouded by dust-covers, hastily whipped off at the appearance of a carriage which might contain a lady. The men whom he invited in after a day's hunting, or who came sometimes to use his father's telescopes, were more comfortable in the library, and it was there that he and Kate always sat.

There was nothing of Kate in this long, impersonal room, with its marble fireplace and glistening chandelier, its fragile furniture covered with pale-tinted brocades. He doubted if she had ever entered it, since the time, long ago, when he had shown her over the whole house. This room was more suited to hold the pale ghost of his mother, or as a background for a woman of detached and studied elegance, a woman such as—Arabella?

Above the tumult of the wind, he heard the carriage drawing up before the door.

Jonathan leaped to the puddled driveway, and put down the steps. Arabella's cloak, escaping her grasp, whipped across his face, knocking off his hat which bowled merrily along the muddy terrace. Clutching his wig, he held back the oath which demanded utterance. He heard Arabella swear softly as she snatched at her cloak and passed into the Manor.

But there was no displeasure on her face or in her voice as she entered the drawing-room and greeted Richard. Again he was momentarily dazzled by her beauty and her air of youthful elegance. He bent over her hand a little too long, so that her father cleared his throat significantly. Arabella smiled into Richard's eyes, and the colour swept into her cheeks as smoothly as a summer wave over sand.

The women he had seen in London were heavily rouged and powdered, with high, fantastic hair styles. He thought her more natural appearance far more alluring.

Arabella, at first so disheartened by her new surroundings that she considered an elaborate toilette a waste of effort, had soon realised it would also be bad taste to employ London habits in the country. By now she had met a few of her nearest neighbours, and her comments upon them in letters to her Aunt Maria were scathing and pithy. But she had the sense to realise that if she were to have any company at all, it was she who must conform. She had also discovered by discreet inquiries that, save for two burly brothers who seemed to bring the stable into the drawing-room, Richard Carryll was the only eligible bachelor in what Arabella referred to as "this savage corner of our country."

If she were forced to accept a countryman as a husband, at least this one had pleasant manners and a certain liveliness of mind.

As Richard greeted her father, Arabella studied the room. The proportions were good, and the furnishings, though out of date, expensive and tasteful. Her mind at once set about improvements.

Richard broke in upon her thoughts. "It was most kind of you to come—to venture out on such a day."

Arabella smiled at him. "I am persuaded, sir, that if one waited for the weather in the country, one would stay abed all day. But I must confess, I thought we should be tipped over more than once on these dreadful roads."

"It is the wagons which cause the ridges," Richard explained seriously. "They are heavily laden, and after the rain—"

"Ah, yes, to be sure. Papa, can you not do something to improve the roads?"

"I scarcely think the turnpike laws have reached here yet. In fact, I doubt if any laws are kept by the inhabitants of this neighbourhood."

Richard, his hand on the bell-rope, hesitated. "Indeed, Sir Henry! You have obtained some proof?"

"Of smuggling activities? Scarcely proof, sir. But, I do not ride with my eyes or ears shut. There have been certain signs, certain peculiarities, I have noticed."

Richard jerked at the rope. He faced Sir Henry, making an effort to appear casual.

"May I inquire what you have discovered?"

The older man's eyes narrowed. He brushed a fleck of soot from his cravat.

"I have always found it the best policy to let as few people as possible know one's movements, or —what one has discovered."

Arabella laughed. "For shame, Papa. One would suppose you believed Mr. Carryll when he said he was a smuggler. I cannot conceive of so—so elegant a gentleman demeaning himself to associate with a lot of rough men in obstructing the law. Although, it would relieve the tedium of life in the country, would it not?"

Richard found two pairs of eyes on him—Arabella's, blue and teasing, her father's opaque, expressionless.

He answered coolly. "But I assure you, I do not find life tedious." Then, to his relief, his housekeeper appeared, followed by a maid with tea.

But Sir Henry would not let the subject rest. He glanced towards the windows as an extra strong gust hurled the cold rain against the glass.

"A south-westerly gale. That means, on this coast, an onshore wind. Dangerous, Mr. Carryll?"

"We are too far up the Chichester channel for it to affect us here, sir, save that a cottage or two may be flooded. You may have observed that some of them have stone walls protecting—"

"Quite. But—the weather would not prevent a boat, a fairly large boat, from coming into the estuary?"

"I think not."

Sir Henry put down his cup and rested his fingertips together. "Indeed? An overcast sky, and the tide full at midnight. A good night, would you say, for—certain operations?"

Arabella sat forward, her wide-eyed gaze moving from her father to Richard. She glanced at the maid. But the girl, as blank-faced as the village women, hovered beside the teapot. Richard motioned her to refill Sir Henry's cup.

"I think the Preventive officers are better able to answer that question than I, sir," he said evenly. "For myself, I favour my bed on such a night."

"The Preventive officers! I believe them to be in league with—" The baronet broke off, realising he had revealed too much. He continued in his cold, precise tones, "You are, in fact, like so many of our countrymen, ready to turn a blind eye to the iniquities that take place all around you."

"There are many who do not consider the traffic in contraband goods a great iniquity, sir."

"My brother amongst them. Charles spoke often in London against the customs laws. He gained no support, and so he came down here to preach his doctrine. Possibly he influenced you, Mr. Carryll?"

Richard was thoughtful. He answered slowly, "No, I cannot say he did, sir."

He congratulated himself that he had evaded the issue by speaking the truth. For it had not been Sir Charles who had influenced him, but Kate. He had listened, good-naturedly but disinterested, while Charles harangued him about the customs laws. Only after Kate had dragged him into the business of freetrading had he realised the opportunity it would give Charles to put his views into practice. But, facing Sir Henry's hard eyes, his rapier-like interrogation, Richard was glad of his years of practice in keeping secrets, in covering up his real thoughts and feelings against those who cared nothing for him.

He asked, as the maid withdrew, "Will you not favour us with some music, Miss Glynde? The spinet has long been unused. But I think you will find it has been put in good order, in the hope that you would play."

She looked at him under her lashes. "You had it looked at—especially for me?"

He rose, bowing low. Standing together beside the spinet, their backs to Sir Henry, they sorted through the sheets of music. For a moment Arabella's fingers touched Richard's with that same butterfly lightness. She heard his indrawn breath, and unobtrusively moved a little closer so that her shoulder was against his arm. He turned to her and she saw wonder in his eyes and then, gradually, something more.

She lowered her lashes and sat demurely on the stool. The fish was nibbling. A little well-chosen music might help to lure him on the hook. She wondered, if once married, he could be persuaded to forsake the country and take a house in London. But first her father must be persuaded that Richard, despite his friendship with Sir Charles, would prove a suitable choice to sire the heir to Falcon Grange.

She planned her arguments as she played, caressing the keys with long, graceful fingers.

Richard's gaze moved from her powdered hair, topped by a tiny white cap, to the curve of her slender neck above the lace of her throat. As she moved, her perfume rose, heavy and piquant. Oblivious of Sir Henry who sat, legs outstretched, fingertips together, staring into the fire, Richard turned the pages of music and felt himself being drawn into a world of magic he had never known existed.

Arabella played three pieces, then made as if to rise. But when Richard pleaded with her to continue, she glanced up, her dimples enchanting him.

"My music-master taught me also to sing. I have so few accomplishments. But music is a delight to me."

"Then will you not allow me to share it?"

"If you wish," she smiled, and held his ardent gaze for a long moment.

She sang softly, in a clear, pure voice which gave to the songs a meaning beyond their words. When the music ended, Richard found himself unable to express his feelings. He murmured a polite remark which he knew to be totally inadequate, and hoped his eyes would tell her the rest.

Sir Henry's dry voice brought a frown to Richard's face.

"You must not weary our host. Though, indeed, you sing quite prettily. I think it is time—"

Richard turned swiftly, searching for an excuse to detain them.

"There are some paintings which are thought tolerably good in the gallery," he suggested. "If you would honour me—"

Arabella, rising from the stool, said quickly, "Papa does not care for paintings. But I would dearly like to see them."

Sir Henry's mouth twitched in the familiar gesture of displeasure as he took out his snuffbox. "You will excuse me, if I remain beside the comfort of your fire?"

Richard bowed, gratified and yet not without a little awe at the prospect of having Arabella to himself.

It was quieter in the long gallery, away from the full force of the gale. Arabella made a pretence of admiring the paintings. As she moved, the full skirt of her black silk dress seemed to glide of its own volition, giving her the dignity of a black swan upon a lake. She paused before the family portraits.

"I apprehend that was your mother? The pale, beautiful girl at the end?"

"Yes. The portrait was painted at the time of her marriage."

"You have her colouring. And—your father?"

As he pointed upwards, she stepped back the better to see. She remarked, on a note of surprise, "Why, he is not unlike my own father. He has the same air of—reserve."

He murmured an acknowledgement, but his heart did not agree. For all his father's asceticism, his scholarly withdrawal from the world and his own son, there was not in his face the cold and calculated cruelty of Sir Henry Glynde.

"He *was* reserved in manner?" Arabella queried.

"He appeared never to recover from the death

of my mother. He was devoted to her. I think he would have preferred me to have died as well."

She laid her hand fleetingly on his sleeve. "Oh, surely not! Our circumstances are oddly similar, Mr. Carryll. My mother was delicate—an invalid for many years. I had little of her company, and both our fathers—"

She turned slightly away and drooped her shoulders. Her voice was so quiet he had to move nearer to hear her.

"I was very lonely as a child. Perhaps—you understand—because you—also—"

He saw her again as when he had taken leave of her at the Grange, so slender and fragile, a creature whom he longed to cherish. He cleared his throat, but his voice was husky.

"Yes. I understand. Because, as you suggest, it is an experience we have shared. I, too, was a very lonely child."

She looked at him over her shoulder, and in her eyes was an expression which made his senses reel. Scarcely knowing what he did, he reached for her hand and pressed his lips upon it. She lowered her lashes to veil the gratification she feared to betray. Gently she withdrew her hand and murmured, "I fear my father will be growing impatient, sir. It was exceedingly kind of you to show me your pictures."

To his enchanted eyes she moved like a princess along the length of the gallery. At the end she turned, mentally planning how she would change the carpet and do away with half the paintings which were outmoded.

But Richard, following her gaze, knew himself a traitor. For this place was filled with memories of the dark-haired, rosy-cheeked child whose throaty laugh had rung out, as together they played hide-and-seek or some other exciting, adventurous game which Kate had invented to while away so many winter's afternoons. And his loneliness had ended with her coming.

7

Jesse Turner grunted as he heaved at the marble slab of the tomb. Matthew Hare, the ostler, pushed back his hat and rubbed a sleeve across his forehead.

" 'Twill be worse getting it back on again," he muttered.

"We should've got more help."

"The fewer folks who know about this, the better," Jesse chuckled, the sound rumbling round the churchyard. "There'll be a row of blank faces, but folks fidgeting a bit, nervous-like, p'raps one or two trying to head off the excisemen. Then, when this tomb is opened, nothing in it! I only hope I'll be around to enjoy the sport."

Throwing back his head, he laughed outright. The ostler said anxiously, "Quiet, Mr. Turner."

Jesse slapped his thigh. "You're too nervous, man. Nothing'll be heard above the wind in these trees."

The rain had died out, but the great elms shadowing the church swayed and groaned, and reluctantly yielded a scatter of leaves and twigs. The candle of the lantern flickered despite the shelter of the sea wall.

Jesse reached into the hollow tomb and brought out a keg of spirits. Turning at a touch on his arm, he found Kate, muffled in her cloak, beside him.

"How long will you be?" she inquired. "I can hear dogs barking as if a stranger is about."

"At this time of night? More like the gale has made the creatures nervous. But we'll not be long. 'Tis but a few steps to your cottage. The ladder is set up?"

"Yes, and the loft prepared. You'd best let Matthew climb up. You have grown heavier of late."

Jesse chuckled as he lifted the keg to his shoulder. "Let us be going," he called to the ostler.

They walked down the path to the gate. Kate paused, "There! Can you not hear the dogs?"

Jesse shook his head. "Your ears are younger than mine, Mistress Kate. I hear only the wind and the sea."

"Perhaps I am mistaken. But I will keep watch outside while you go in."

The wind played its tumultuous symphony, crashing out bass chords as it swept along the alleys, using the trees as stringed instruments, rattling windows like drums. The sea pounded out its changeless rhythm against the protecting wall of the harbour. Clutching her cloak tightly around her, straining her ears for any unfamiliar sound, Kate exulted in this display of nature's power. Yet, it had been such a night, she recollected, when her father's ship, blown off course, had foundered on the Selsey peninsula.

She shivered. It would not do to let her mind stray to disasters.

The two men came out of the cottage.

"You were right about the ladder, Mistress Kate,"

Jesse laughed. " 'Twas made for a lightweight. All quiet?"

"As quiet as this night can be. But I am uneasy. Be as quick as you can."

The men went off to the churchyard. Suddenly, in a momentary lull in the wind, Kate heard a cough from the darkness opposite. She froze against the wall, her mouth dry. The cough was repeated, followed by a scraping sound as of a nailed boot dragging on stone. Then the roar of the wind drowned all else.

What should she do? Remain flattened against the wall, waiting for the unknown prowler to appear? Or try to gain the churchyard and warn the men? For long seconds she hesitated, cursing now the clamour of the gale.

Then she realised that if it were a stranger in the shadows opposite, the dogs would give warning. But the barking had ceased. Who, then?

With a rush of pity, she knew. Only poor Jamie, ejected from the one-roomed cottage which was his home, to spend the night in whatever shelter he could find, while his mother "entertained."

Kate sighed, the sound a mixture of relief and regret. The kegs of spirits would be housed more comfortably than the lame boy.

The men returned, carried in more kegs, and disappeared again into the darkness. Kate, relaxing, thought of Richard. There had been no opportunity to consult him about this operation. Besides, he would disapprove of her hiding contraband goods in her cottage. He would have thought out a more elaborate plan. But she and Jesse had agreed that the kegs must be moved at once, after Arabella

Glynde had taken such interest in the unfrequented part of the churchyard.

The cottage door creaked as the men passed inside. When they emerged, Jesse's loud whisper sounded in her ear.

"Mistress Judith is calling you."

"She is so frightened of storms. I had hoped she would remain asleep. How many more barrels to fetch?"

"About a half-dozen."

She felt herself buffeted, as the trees were, this way and that. She was pledged to help the free-traders. Yet Judith needed her. The pathetic cripple, crouched on his doorstep, cried out to her conscience. And when she met Richard, he would look at her with gentle disapproval over this night's doings, and she would become angry in self-defence, and regret it afterwards. She tapped her foot on the doorstep, willing the men to hurry, impatient for some action to release the tension of her thoughts.

She heard Judith's cry, and knew she could no longer leave such an appeal unanswered. She had but to fail the girl once, and all the past months' efforts would have been in vain.

Kate's hand was on the latch when the clamour of barking dogs broke out along the street.

From the shadows opposite a man emerged. He came straight towards her. Hand against mouth, she pressed back against the wall. The man came on. She wanted to scream for help; yet knew she must not. Somehow she must give Jesse and Matthew warning. The stranger stopped no more than two feet away from her.

Judith cried out again, shrill above the wind.

The man took another step, raised his hand. Kate, cursing the impeding folds of her cloak, lunged forward. Desperately she pummelled at the stranger's chest. She heard him gasp as he tripped and fell backwards.

Then the smugglers were upon him. In a moment he was gagged and bound.

Kate, quickly recovering, whispered, "Bandage his eyes with a kerchief, and bring him inside. It is too dark to see who he is. Besides, we do not want the whole village aroused."

They dragged their captive into her parlour, while she lit candles. Jesse caught him by the throat.

"Are there any more with you?"

The man shook his head. Kate bent over him, candle in hand. Her startled gaze took in the blue breeches and coat, faced with yellow, his white cotton stockings and black shoes, the powdered wig askew on his cropped head.

"We have caught a pretty fish, indeed," she said. "This young man wears the livery of Sir Henry Glynde."

The ostler whistled through his teeth. "Then we had better stain it for him."

Kate thrust out a hand. "No. He is but a youth. Take out his gag and let us question him."

Into the taut silence that filled the little room, Judith's scream broke like shattered glass. The young man struggled to sit up.

"Will none of you go to her?" he demanded. "Have you no heart—you, who have the voice of a woman—to leave such a cry unanswered?"

He fought against Jesse's restraining arms. The breath all but knocked out of him, he croaked, "Judith! Judith!"

Wide-eyed, Kate stared at him. Suddenly she saw, not the dishevelled figure lying on the floor, but a young man leaping from a coach.

"Your name is Jonathan?" she asked.

"Yes. But—"

"Be still. I am going to her." Her hand on the stair-rail, Kate turned to Jesse. "I will not be long. But if either of you harm a hair of this man's head—"

They looked away, as did her pupils when they saw that expression in her eyes. She bounded upstairs and into Judith's room, gathering the girl into her arms in a passion of self-reproach.

"It—it seemed as though I was alone in the world," Judith sobbed. "There was so much noise, I feared you would never hear me. I tried to find my way to you. But I fell, and then I did not know where I was. It was like a nightmare—only I was awake."

"It is but the gale. There is nothing to fear."

After a few minutes Judith murmured. "I am ashamed to be so fearful. I am no longer a child, who cannot reason—"

"You cannot reason against the terror that comes with darkness, not yet. You have too many times known your fears well-founded."

While she soothed Judith, feeling the trembling of her body gradually pass away, Kate was in a turmoil to know what was going on downstairs. She longed to tell Judith that the young man who had snatched her from beneath the horses' hooves was still concerned for her. How it would divert the girl's mind from these phantom terrors which came with the night. But Jonathan's purpose in coming so stealthily to the village had yet to be discovered.

Judith fingered Kate's clothes. "You are wearing your cloak! You have been out—on such a night?"

"I thought I heard a child crying," she thought up on the spur of the moment. "I went outside to see."

"And did you find one?"

"No. It was but Jamie, sleeping in a doorway."

"You will not leave him there? You will fetch him in, as you did me?"

"His mother will beat him if I do."

"You will stop her. You are strong enough to do anything, Kate."

She started to protest. But suddenly she saw this as an excuse to leave Judith without causing suspicion in her mind. If the girl were questioned, she must know nothing of this night's happenings. Gently she disengaged herself and tucked in the bed-clothes.

"I will fetch Jamie. You will not be afraid any more?"

"Not if I know you will come back. You must go to that poor boy."

"I may be a little while. Cover your ears and try to sleep."

When she went downstairs, Kate found Jonathan sitting on an upright chair, his arms pinioned behind him, the kerchief still binding his eyes. There was an uneasy silence in the room.

Kate motioned to the kegs standing beside the door, and pointed upstairs. Matthew frowned. But Jesse walked across and hoisted a barrel to his shoulder.

"Not you," Kate said. "It is better that you keep

104

watch outside while—while he," she gestured towards the ostler, "goes aloft. And stays there," she added severely, "until I call."

Jesse nodded and, passing the key to Matthew, went outside. Experience had taught him to trust this girl's wits. But the ostler was new to the district and did not take kindly to accepting orders from a woman. Seeing him hesitate, Kate said fiercely, "You would murder him out of hand, no doubt. But I think to have other means of persuasion. Get you aloft."

The ladder creaked as he mounted. Kate scraped a chair across the floor to cover the sound.

Jonathan had ceased his struggles. But he strained forwards, his body rigid.

"You—you are going to kill me?" he whispered.

"Is there good reason why we should?"

"I do not understand."

"Why are you in the village, at so late an hour, on the night of a full gale? Answer me that, and I will tell you if it is necessary for you to—disappear."

"I cannot answer. I am sworn to secrecy."

"By whom? Your master?"

He nodded.

"Ah! So it *was* Sir Henry Glynde who sent you? For what purpose?"

The set of his jaw was stubborn.

"You will not tell me? The sea is a cold grave, Master Jonathan."

Still he remained silent. Kate brought a candle nearer his face. She saw he was no older than herself. Again she questioned him.

"Sir Henry imposes the threat of death for disobedience—is that it?"

She knew by the jerk of his head that she was right. She put down the candlestick and, glancing upstairs to make sure Matthew was out of sight, untied the kerchief from Jonathan's eyes.

He blinked at her. "*You* are Dame Hardham?"

"I am. Doubtless you thought to find an old woman to overpower."

Dazedly he shook his head. Kate spoke quietly.

"Listen to me. You are the footman who saved Judith's life?"

"Possibly I did, but—"

"This is no time for mock modesty. Just now you called her name, and were concerned because you thought her in distress. Why?"

"*Why?*" He lunged forwards, tipping the chair. "Have you a heart of stone—that you leave her to wander alone and helpless on the roads, and do not answer when she cries out to you?"

"You would be anxious, then, if Judith were in danger?"

"I would give my life to prevent it."

"You care so much—when you did but see her for a few moments?"

"It was enough."

She turned away, so that she should not betray her feelings. She spoke harshly. "If you would save her from harm, you will tell me why you are in the village."

Straining against his bonds, he looked as if he would hurl himself at her.

"You would torture her? You would do *that*— to get your way?"

Kate whirled to face him. "*Torture* her? What nonsense are you speaking? You think that *I* would harm her?"

"Why not? Have you not already done so, this very night?"

She rested her hands on his shoulders, looking deep into his hostile eyes.

"You must believe me, Jonathan. Judith was not in pain. She was but frightened of the storm. I should have gone to her before, had you not come creeping like a thief into our village. It is not I who will harm her. It is you."

"How can that be?"

"By the tale you take back to your master—of what you have seen and heard. You have but to say that you were kidnapped into this house, to set the law in action. Men such as your master have no pity, Jonathan. The fact that Judith is blind, and was abed, will not save her. Even if it did, but I am taken, where does she turn for shelter? She has nobody to care for her. Nobody but me —and you."

He felt the power in the small hands on his shoulders. He was held by the dark eyes searching his own. His brain felt clouded over. He was not sure she spoke the truth.

He had a choice, it seemed, of death here in this cottage, and afterwards his body tossed into the raging sea; or death by some trumped-up charge because he had disobeyed his master. He knew the power of men such as Sir Henry Glynde. They could break a man by a word; have him transported for life for the merest crime. Further to confuse him, this masterful woman was suggesting he offered a threat to the blind girl who had so immediately captured his heart.

While he was trying to order his thoughts, Kate spoke again.

"I do not want to see you harmed. You saved Judith, whom I hold as dear as a sister. Will you not save her again—and yourself?"

"But how? I see no way."

"Why did you come here tonight?"

He closed his eyes. He saw the face of his master, thin-lipped as he uttered his threat. "If you so much as breathe a word of my orders—" He saw Judith's face, white and frightened, against his shoulder, then suddenly trusting as he spoke to her.

When he opened his eyes again, the girl who seemingly held his life in her hands no longer appeared threatening. Her face was full of pleading, so that she looked younger than he had previously thought.

Swallowing hard, he said slowly, "I was ordered to stand all night beneath the trees where the road around the estuary joins the one to Chichester. I was to watch and listen, and to report to Sir Henry any strange happening."

Kate's eyes widened. "What did you think to learn?"

"I was not told. But, since my master has been a magistrate and I have heard there is smuggling in these parts—"

"What did you see?"

"Why, nothing, mistress. And the wind in the trees drowned any other sound."

"Of course. Your master is a fool. So—you could truthfully report to him that, while you watched, nothing untoward occurred on the Chichester road tonight?"

Jonathan's face began to clear. "Yes. I could do that."

"Nothing did happen at the place you should

have watched, I promise you. But you left your post. Why?"

He shuffled his feet, hung his head. Kate questioned him again.

Flushing, he mumbled, "You will think it foolish. I had already been into the village and learned where Judith lived. The thought came to me to—to—"

"To come *here*—in the middle of the night? For what purpose?"

He moved uneasily. "Only to stand, across the street, and know I was near her."

Astonished into silence, Kate stared at him. Matthew's whisper came down the stairs.

"Are you all right, mistress?"

Jonathan turned his head. Kate stepped quickly to hide his view of the stairs.

"Give me a few moments more," she called. She went on with her questions.

"When you stood there, you saw—what?"

"Nothing—save a boy sleeping in a doorway."

"You did not know I was by the wall?"

"That I did not. The first I knew was when you came for me. Then something hit me from behind."

"But you raised your arm."

"To strike upon the door—to rouse somebody to answer Judith's call—or break it down if need be."

"It seems you are a man of some spirit, Master Jonathan. Are you also a good liar?"

"I can be—if so be a lie is called for."

"Then you will practise the art. You will tell Sir Henry Glynde that you neither slept nor strayed from your post, and you saw—"

"Nothing, mistress," he broke in. "Nothing at all."

109

He smiled at her, hopefully. She untied the rope which bound him to the chair. He chafed his wrists, then bent to loose his legs. The chair scraped on the floor as he rose, stamping to restore the circulation.

Quick as a monkey, the ostler leapt down the stairs. He crouched, knife in hand, ready to spring. Too startled for a moment to think, Kate stared at the two men. Then she flung herself in front of Jonathan, arms outstretched.

"You fool! I told you—there were other means than violence. Now, whereas before he had but heard your voice, he has seen your face."

Matthew stood uncertain, his fingers caressing the handle of his knife.

"*You* unbound him—took the bandage from his eyes?" he exclaimed.

"I did. He is to go free."

Matthew's eyes glinted as he moved forward.

"Dead men cannot speak of what they have seen."

"This man will not speak, I promise you."

"On what guarantee?"

"His word—and my belief that he will keep it."

Matthew spat contemptuously into the grate. "A woman's trust—based on nothing. You had best let me deal with this. Move aside, mistress."

Jonathan gripped Kate's shoulders, trying to put her behind him. But she stood her ground, scornfully facing the ostler.

"Come then, you who are so brave, so anxious to kill an unarmed man."

Matthew weaved from side to side, seeking a way to pass her. Suddenly Jonathan grasping her by the waist, heaved her aside. She fell against the door.

"I will not hide behind a woman's skirts," he exclaimed. Fists clenched, he fronted Matthew. "Now come on, though I do not know what quarrel you have with me."

Kate wrenched open the door. Seizing Jesse's arm, she dragged him inside.

"Stop him! For pity's sake, stop him!"

Jesse strode across the room. Gripping Matthew's wrist in his huge hand, he sent the knife clattering on the floor.

"What madness is this?" he demanded. "If there is need to kill a man, you do it quietly, beneath a hedge where none shall see or hear. Not like this, where he has but to shout to wake the neighbourhood, and before a woman—"

He turned to Kate. "How did he get free? He was securely bound."

"I freed him."

"You had good reason?"

"Yes. If this fool had not bounded down the stairs like a madman, Jonathan would have seen no other face but mine. As it is—" She shrugged. Turning to Jonathan, she said, "I fear it is out of my hands. I did my best for you."

"I would not have betrayed you. I would have kept my word, because—" He glanced up the stairs, sadness in his face.

Jesse turned to Kate, his great bulk dominating the room. "You see fit to let him go?"

"I do. A man does not willingly let another destroy that which he loves."

"You speak in riddles, Mistress Kate. But I never had cause to doubt your judgement." He pointed to the door, addressing Jonathan. "Go now. But if you show your face here again—"

Kate laid a hand on the young man's arm. "Keep

your word," she said quietly, "and I will find a way—for you to speak with Judith."

Joy broke across his troubled face like sunlight over a shadowed lake.

"God bless you, mistress. I will keep my word, never fear."

He went through the door without another glance at the two men. The candles flickered in the draught.

Kate said wearily, "There are still more kegs to fetch?"

Jesse shook his head. "Not here. The rest can go into my cellar. Shall I move the ladder?"

Suddenly she wanted to end the whole business. "I can deal with that. I will keep watch for you, and then—"

Jesse picked up the ropes which had bound Jonathan. "We'll manage. Two journeys will see it finished. Matthew, take that surly look off your face, and come with me. It is time you learned there are occasions when a woman's wits are better than violence. I've been in the trade ten years and never killed a man yet, though I've witnessed it. And I am still alive and free."

The ostler thrust the knife back into his belt.

"Then you won't be for long, after this night's madness. You risk the gibbet for smuggling, as we all do. What does it matter if you throw in a murder for good measure?"

"I will tell you," Kate answered. "In the words of the man who was our friend and whom we all trusted—Sir Charles Glynde, 'Break the law of man,' he said, 'and you are answerable to man. But take a man's life, and you will answer to God.'"

Matthew shuffled his feet, refusing to meet her

eyes. Jesse pushed him through the door. They hesitated a moment, looking up and down the street. Then they set out once more for the church-yard.

Jesse's chuckle flew away on the wind. "Do not be so glum, Matthew. Mistress Kate has overridden better men than you. I know no braver or finer woman—no, not even my wife."

Sulkily, nursing his hurt pride, Matthew trudged along in the darkness. But he was the newest member of the band of freetraders. And there was one rule which was never broken, the rule of loyalty.

Kate, hurrying after them to remind them they had left one keg in her parlour, was only a step behind when he gave his answer.

"I'll allow she's a brave enough wench. Handsome too, in her way. But I'd not be the husband of Kate Hardham for all the silver in Christendom."

8

Richard sipped his wine in the hall of Falcon Grange nervously smoothing his cravat. For the twentieth time he glanced at his new breeches, wondering if their cut, designed for the country, would appear inelegant to Arabella. The gallants who had surrounded her, that evening in London, had been gaudy as peacocks, their ruffles of finest lace, their hair elaborately curled and powdered. Here in Sussex, one dressed for comfort. A day's hunting would plaster a pair of breeches with sticky mud; a morning's shooting jag the finest broadcloth, or leave a wig strung ludicrously upon a branch.

He looked up at the portrait of Sir Charles—a man who had dressed as he pleased, acted as he pleased; a man big enough to defy conventions and yet beloved and respected wherever he went. He looked alive enough to step down from the wall and fill this house again with his rumbustious presence.

Richard found the stillness oppressive. Even the logs were burning slowly, reluctantly, without the gaiety of sparks. The young footman who stood discreetly by the door, stifled a yawn behind his white-gloved hand. The house appeared to have taken on the character of its new owner.

Richard emptied his glass and began to pace the room, hands behind his back. He felt edgy with lack of sleep. The gale had rattled his windows, roared down his chimney. He had tossed and turned, his mind in as much turmoil as the night. Around his bed had stood three figures. Arabella, fair, elegantly beautiful, beckoning with a white finger, smiling the while her eyes mocked him: Kate, with dark head bent in silent reproach for a promise he had so lightly given, and the menacing figure of Sir Henry Glynde, his secrets hidden behind the bloodless mask of his face.

Richard stopped his pacing and stood again before the portrait.

"Why did you have to die?" he questioned silently, as Arabella had done before him. "Yet, if you had not—I should not be waiting now, my heart in my mouth—for Arabella."

He turned at a sound. He gained the foot of the stairs as Arabella reached the landing. She paused, moving her body slightly so that the sunlight caressed with golden ripples the black velvet of her riding-habit, and made a dazzling halo of her hair beneath her black tricorne.

Gratified by his stillness and the admiration in his eyes, she descended the last flight, seeming to float on air so that he all but held out his arms to catch her. Always he had seen her with light emphasising her beauty, candle-light on pale shoulders, firelight shining into her blue eyes, and now the sun irradiating the slender lines of her body.

Feeling a lump in his throat, he bent over her hand, murmuring incoherent words of greeting. He felt so encompassed in a magic world which contained only themselves, that when she spoke to the footman, he was startled.

"I will not take any wine, Jonathan. It seems that Sussex can provide some sun and warmth after all. I wish to take advantage of it."

Pulling on her gloves, she turned to Richard. "My father begs that you will excuse him. He is closeted with his notary. It appears that some of my uncle's affairs are not entirely straightforward. There are certain payments, and letters, over which my father is somewhat at a loss. Not understanding French, he asked me to translate them, and—"

"*French!*" Richard almost choked on the word.

Arabella looked faintly surprised, "Is it so strange that my uncle should have correspondence with France? I confess the letters did not make sense to me. There were references to moonlight, and 'pretty darlings.' " Her laughter rippled out. "It would seem, almost, that my uncle kept a harem of young French misses."

Richard gave her a wan smile. "You do him an injustice."

She shrugged her delicate shoulders. "Oh, I think not. He had no wife. One would not expect him to live like a monk. Were there not often ladies at the Grange?"

"I never saw them."

Her eyes flicked up at him with the mockery he found so tantalising. "You are discreet, sir, and loyal. They are traits I much admire."

He bowed, and followed her from the hall. But as he left, he threw a glance over his shoulder at the massive door of the library, wishing his eyes could bore holes to reveal what dangerous secrets lay beyond.

Charles had been careless in many ways. He would forget where he tossed his purse; he forbade his housekeeper to lock her cupboards. He trusted his servants as he trusted his friends, and all of them knew of his support for the freetraders. But —to leave incriminating papers for any eye to light on? Surely he would not have committed such folly? Yet, he had not expected to die, so suddenly, without warning. How could he have known that strangers would come into his house, or that his own brother would poke and pry into every corner, sniffing like a ferret into holes which should have been stopped up?

Arabella, from the mounting-block, remarked, "You seem a little distrait this morning, Mr. Carryll. Did the gale, after all, disturb your rest?"

"I—I beg your pardon." He made an effort to account for his preoccupation. "The fact is, your —your beauty so overwhelmed me that it drove out any other thought."

Leaning from the saddle, she tapped him lightly on the shoulder with her crop. "A gallant speech.

116

I was tempted to suppose that you were disappointed that my father is unable to accompany us—that you would find my company tedious."

He took his mare's reins from the groom. "Indeed not," he assured her with such warmth that she laughed at him over her shoulder as she urged her horse forward.

They rode through the park, the groom discreetly out of earshot. The deer lifted startled heads from their grazing and bounded away on slender legs. In a clump of tall trees, herons stood sentinel beside their nests. A blue haze foretold the birth of bluebells amongst the delicate blush of wood anemones. Bird-song was the only sound to break the hushed stillness of the morning.

Richard sighed with contentment. This was the country he knew and loved; the sun was warm upon his back, the excitement of spring surging through his veins. Beside him rode a girl as enchanting as any pictures conjured up by reading or by dreams.

Arabella pointed with her whip to where, in the distance, the forest ended and a line of green hills rose, nebulous, into the pale blue sky.

"Are those the mountains through which we passed on our journey from London? They appear less menacing this morning."

Richard could not restrain a laugh. "Mountains? They are but gentle slopes, I do assure you. Your horse could climb them in an hour."

She gave an exaggerated shudder. "I have no wish to leave the level ground. Indeed, it is wild enough here. Such wastes of lonely country frighten me."

Astonished, he stared at her. "But it is not wild

or lonely here. See, here is Altonlea Hall through the trees, and over the stream there is a farmhouse, and beyond, a cottage."

"But surely people who live in such isolation must be—at least, Mr. Horace Walpole says they are—" She broke off, observing the hardening of his face.

"Savages? No, they are quite civilised. Not versed in the classics, perhaps, but worthy men and women, nevertheless, attending church on the Sabbath—"

"And smuggling the rest of the week?" she laughed, seeking to divert him from his earnestness.

He frowned; then quickly recovered himself. "No doubt. Perhaps even now, there is a dangerous fellow lurking in the wood yonder, ready to guard his secret hideout against our prying gaze."

Her horse threw up its head as she jerked at the bridle.

"I will go no farther," she declared, her eyes dark in her pale face. "Pray escort me home at once."

Richard reached across and took her reins. "I was but teasing you, ma'am. Pray forgive me. I forget that the country is strange to you, that you are more accustomed to ride in the Park, surrounded by people and carriages. Believe me, there is no danger."

She laid her hand upon his sleeve. The tremor of her fingers filled him with a desire to protect her. He upbraided himself for causing her anxiety.

He said huskily, "Did you think it possible, that I would risk any harm to so fair a jewel entrusted to my care?"

She gave him a long, intense look, which sent a tingling sensation up his spine.

"Indeed, I think the country cannot be so wild, sir, since it produces so exquisite a turn of phrase."

For a moment, she allowed her fingers to rest upon his hand as she took up her reins. He would have imprisoned them. But once again, her eyes mocked him. Moving forward, she said, "Let us be going on our way to Chichester. My groom will be putting a strange construction upon this halt."

They came presently to a farm gate. Waiting for her groom to open it, Arabella caught sight of a family of piglets and exclaimed in delight. But a moment later, she put a hand to her mouth, her eyes wide.

"We are not going through that yard, past those —those creatures?"

Richard turned to discover the cause of her fear.

"Why not? They are but cows."

"But—they stare so. I am persuaded they mean us harm."

Smiling as tolerantly as he would at a frightened child, he reassured her. "They are merely curious. I do assure you, they will not even move as we pass."

He rode between her and the cows, while her horse sweated with nervousness and Arabella did not take her eyes from the placid creatures following her movements with such a steady, concentrated gaze.

Sighing with relief when they reached the safety of the farther gate, demurely she looked up at Richard.

"You will think me foolish, sir. I crave your indulgence for my weakness."

His eyes were tender as he smiled at her. She made him feel twice his normal size. He wished himself back in the days of medieval chivalry when he could have worn her favour upon his lance as

119

he entered the lists, and claimed her admiration as he tossed into the dust some knight famed for his prowess.

Ten minutes later, he was given the opportunity to play the gallant.

Arabella rode close beside him over an open stretch of grassland. Then they entered a wood and were forced to adopt single file along the narrow path. She called up her groom to protect her from any unknown dangers which might threaten her from behind. Even then, she glanced into the undergrowth on either side. She transmitted her nervousness to her horse.

A wood pigeon clattered noisily from a branch above her head. Her mount shied violently. Finding itself hemmed in, unable to bolt, the animal reared and plunged. Its nostrils distended, a lather of sweat along its neck, its hooves crashed down, trampling the wild flowers.

Richard, a few yards ahead, turned at the commotion. Arabella, white-faced, was struggling for control. A voice inside Richard's head urged, "Do something." But the familiar numbness of brain had him in its grip—the inability to make a quick decision in the face of emergency.

By the time he had shaken it off and moved forward, the groom had settled the matter for him. Jumping to the ground, he ran behind the trees. Gaining the frightened animal's head, he grabbed the reins, bringing it under control.

Richard, standing in his stirrups, retrieved Arabella's hat from a branch.

"You are a splendid horsewoman, ma'am."

"It seems I need to be, sir. Pray, what other hazards do I face before we reach Chichester?"

Furious with himself for his failure to assist her before the groom came to her rescue, Richard spoke sharply.

"None, I trust. Nor would the flight of a bird have been one, had you chosen a horse from Sir Charles's stable. Your mount is better suited to performing a caracole in a London park."

She paused in the act of pinning on her hat, a biting retort on her lips. But she checked herself.

"I concede you are right," she murmured sweetly. "I should have allowed you to advise me, who know this neighbourhood so well."

He gave a stiff little bow. "Is it your wish that we return to the Grange?"

She took her reins from the silent groom and straightened her shoulders.

"No. We will proceed, since I am assured of ample protection. Nor am I so easily defeated, Mr. Carryll."

He wondered, as he rode before her, what was behind her words. He had thought it simple to understand this girl. She was young, lonely in these unfamiliar surroundings. Her father could scarcely provide the lively company she obviously craved.

He had felt tender and protective towards her. But now, suddenly, there was steel in her voice, a challenge in her eyes. For the first time he regretted his inexperience. For what had Kate taught him of women? Kate, who was forthright and never dissembled, and was as far removed from this elegant creature as a lively unbroken colt from a perfectly mannered thoroughbred.

Arabella, forgetful now of any imaginary dangers threatening from the wood, rode with a little smile of satisfaction playing round her mouth. She had thought that her wooing of this earnest young man would be exceedingly dull. A lift of her finger, and he would come running. She had been bored by his naïve compliments, by his talk of estate matters and the chase, and his ignorance of the London life which was the only one she desired.

But he had not rushed, all anxious devotion, to her aid. He had left the matter very properly to her groom, and confined himself to the more dignified effort of retrieving her hat. Then he had criticised her and withdrawn stiffly into his shell.

His back spoke volumes to her. She had thought to have him at her feet within a week; to be betrothed to him as soon as her period of mourning ended; to be his wife in time to persuade him to take a house in London for the winter. She had thought the only problem was her father.

But Richard's back suggested that her conquest would not be so easy. So much the better. After the years of her father's domination, she did not intend to submit to any other man. But a husband without some spirit would be exceedingly dull.

Betsy Turner's dimpled hand twirled the smooth surface of the globe. Triumphantly she jabbed a finger.

"There! That's England, that little bit!"

Her face fell as Kate gave her only a curt nod. It was not often Betsy gave sufficient attention to her lessons even to answer a question. When she answered correctly she expected applause. She pouted, and pointed to America.

"I can show you where the New World is, too."

"Good. And now, Van Dieman's Land."

Kate was giving but half her mind to Betsy's attempts at geography. She was trying to listen to the whispering which was going on behind her back as she stood at the window. She caught Willy's scornful words.

". . . by keeping your eyes open. The grass is trampled, and there are footprints on the earth."

He was answered by a treble squeak. "But the Squire's daughter walked that way—and Dame Hardham."

"Women have small feet, you oaf! These were men's prints. I wonder if parson knows there are other things than corpses buried in the churchyard. Perhaps I'll tell him."

"You wouldn't dare!"

"Wouldn't I? You'll see."

Betsy pointed hopefully to Spain and announced she had found Van Dieman's Land. Kate said impatiently. "No. You do not attend, child. William will show you."

The lengthening of his name warned Willy that trouble was afoot. He murmured anxiously. "Show her what, ma'am?"

"Where it is—on the globe."

"Where—where what is?"

"So Betsy is not the only one who does not listen." Kate rapped him smartly across the knuckles with her birch. "I have warned you before, that your tongue is too long. Keep it locked behind your teeth, save when you are asked to speak."

But Willy, since it was his ambition to impress the blue-eyed Betsy, put his head on one side and answered cheekily. "And if I am asked questions, ma'am? By the excisemen, say?"

Startled, she exclaimed, "They have been here?"

"I have not seen them, ma'am. But my grandfather says, now we have a Squire who has been a magistrate, it is likely they *will* come."

"And of all the village, they will pick on you as the most likely, intelligent boy to question?"

Willy reddened as laughter ran round the schoolroom. Betsy clapped her plump hands together in delight. Willy thrust out his chin.

"They would be sensible if they did. There is much I could tell them."

"Indeed! That you have heard tales of what happened in your grandfather's day; that there are signs that people have wandered from the paths in the churchyard, that—"

Galled by the sarcasm in her tone, he interrupted, "More than that. I would tell them all I saw—"

"Well?" prompted Kate, as he broke off. "All you saw—when?"

He hung his head, realising he had gone too far. Kate followed up her advantage.

"One night when you were supposed to be in bed, is that it? Or was it that you ate too big a supper, and dreamed it all?"

He sat hunched up, his face flushed but stubborn, while the guffaws sounded all around him.

"Such dreams are foolish," Kate said quietly. "Foolish, Willy, and dangerous. This is my last warning to you. If you do not curb your tongue, I will do it for you."

She moved towards the fireplace. Willy, with a startled glance at the poker, scrambled from his seat and raced for the door. They heard his shout, followed by a cry of pain, and the thud of some object falling on the ground.

Kate, looking out of the window, saw Willy dart

124

into an alley. Below her, Jamie lay sprawled, rubbing his leg.

Going to the door, she called, "Are you hurt?"

"Not much. He knocked me over." The boy raised himself awkwardly on to his leg, watching her anxiously.

"What were you doing there, Jamie, beside my window? This is not the first time I have found you so."

"I—I was just resting. I meant no harm."

Puzzled, she frowned at him. "But why do you not find a bench, or even the stone wall by the harbour? You would get the sun there. It is cold here at this time of day."

He dusted himself down and tucked the crutch beneath his arm. He started off along the street, shoulders sagging, his ungainly progress followed by a group of jeering children in a doorway. He had gone but a few yards when Kate called him back. As he looked at her with soft brown eyes, she was reminded of the hopeless expression in the eyes of a dog she had once found being stoned from the village.

"Wait in the back parlour," she told him. "I will come to you when lessons are ended."

He cast a fearful glance towards his mother's cottage. Kate put a hand on his bony shoulder.

"Do as I tell you, Jamie," she said gently. "No harm will come to you, I promise."

With the air of a cowed puppy he followed her, and sat down obediently on the chair she pulled up to the fire. She saw his eyes fixed longingly on a tray of tarts on the table.

"Have you had anything to eat since the bread and milk I gave you at daybreak?"

125

Shaking his head, he swallowed hard against the savoury odours of cooking food, which made his mouth water. Kate put two tarts on a plate beside him.

"It is not long before we have our meal. But you may have these now. I trust you to take no more."

Dumbly, he reached out a tentative hand. His fingers closed over a tart. But his eyes never left her face. They looked enormous above the shadowed hollows of his cheeks.

A commotion in the schoolroom made her exclaim with annoyance.

"I must go. Judith will be returning soon. Say to her that I told you to stay here, and that you are to share our dinner."

She did not know if he understood. The manner in which he cowered in the chair, gripping the tart as if he expected it to be wrenched from him, reminded her of Judith in those first distrustful weeks. Closing the door on him, she stood a moment, fighting the rush of bitter pity which engulfed her. She wished she could have before her all those who reduced children to such a state. Her hand clenched on an imaginary horse-whip, knowing she could wield it with the strength of anger. Then, sighing, she went into the schoolroom to try patiently to coax another correct answer from the innkeeper's spoiled daughter.

She was met by two rows of curious eyes, a subdued silence. For the next half-hour she had the children's whole attention. She wished that Willy, who caused so much disturbance, could be removed altogether; yet in geography and arithmetic he was her most promising pupil. If only he would confine his lively intelligence within safe bounds.

She determined to speak to his father when he returned, with unladen packhorses and silver in his pocket, from London.

By the time the books were put away and chairs straightened, Judith had set the table and cut bread and cheese. She stood over Jamie, holding her nose.

"I am trying to persuade him to wash. He says Willy knocked him down. He must have fallen into some noxious—"

"You are right. He smells like a farmyard. Be off with you to the pump. There is soap beside it."

He limped away, to return a few minutes later with streaks of black where he had simply sluiced his face with grubby hands. Kate, stirring a pot of soup, exclaimed in exasperation.

"Will I take a scrubbing-brush to you, boy? 'Tis your hair which gives most offence. Come with me."

He ducked. But Kate was too quick for him. Seizing him by the back of his neck she forced him, hopping, across the yard. Vigorously she applied soap and water while he worked the pump handle, gasping and spluttering in useless protest. At last she was satisfied and let him stand upright, to lean against the wall. Handing him a towel, she gave him a light slap on the back, like an ostler patting a horse after grooming.

Stifling a cry, the boy cringed, stumbled, and would have fallen had she not caught his arm.

"But that could not have hurt, child. I did but tap your shoulder blade."

His face twisted in pain. He bit his lip. A moment longer Kate stared, mystified. Then she tugged his shirt from his trousers, pulling it up to his neck.

Across his back, where the ribs made a pattern like the bones of a dead ship, red weals striped white skin. Congealed blood was crusted along the ridges. Over his kidneys were the sullen purple and yellow hues of bruising.

Not trusting herself to speak, Kate pulled down the boy's shirt and, giving him her arm, supported him back to the cottage. There she set a bowl of soup before him. Before she and Judith had finished breaking bread into their own, his bowl was empty. Silently she refilled it, and averted her eyes, finding unbearable the way he clutched his bowl and spoon and gulped down the soup with the wariness of an animal expecting its meal to be snatched away. Judith spoke to him, gently, several times. But he spared no breath to answer her. When the meal was over he watched, fascinated, as she cleared the table, her sensitive fingers moving, exploratory, over the cloth, her steps firm as she walked straight to the kitchen sink.

Kate, searching in a cupboard, said, "Take off your shirt, Jamie."

He leapt up, grabbing his crutch. He had gained the door by the time Kate realised what was happening. She was beside him as he fumbled with the latch. Seeing escape impossible, he flattened himself against the wall and stared at her with wide eyes in which terror struggled with unbelief.

"I am not going to beat you, child." She showed him the jar of unguent. "This is to spread on those sore places on your back. See, I will rub some on my own hand, so that you will know it does not hurt."

He watched silently as the white salve disappeared under her gentle massage. When he raised his eyes again, they were puzzled but unafraid.

"Now, will you take off your shirt?"

He nodded, hobbled to the bench, and stripped. He sat hunched forward, patiently enduring, while she applied the healing balm to the ugly weals, and it was she who flinched as she touched the tenderest spots.

Afterwards, he sat before the fire, following with his spaniel gaze her every movement as she poured water from the great black kettle and washed the dishes, while Judith wiped. He listened to their talk. But presently the comfort of a full stomach and a warm fire was too much for him. Resting his elbows on the table, he fell asleep.

"You will not turn him out, Kate?" Judith whispered.

"Not unless his mother shouts for him. Perhaps, if she is getting sufficient money from the sailor who is her present paramour, she can do without Jamie's stealing. But whether she will feed or shelter him—"

"Could you not take him in, as you did me? I— I would work harder at my baskets and knitting, to help pay for his food."

Kate put an arm round the girl's shoulders. "When God took away your sight, child, he doubled the size of your heart. I cannot take Jamie as I took you. He has a mother, slut though she is. When her trade is slack she counts on Jamie to beg or steal enough to fill her days with drinking until the next man comes along. She would not let him go, unless—" She paused, an idea forming in her mind. "There may be a way. I must talk to Richard."

His name hung in the silence. Suddenly she wanted him, with all her being, remembering with what tenderness he had held her, telling her at last that he loved her.

The blind girl for whom she had accepted responsibility; the sleeping boy now trusting her. The dangerous contents of her loft, and the pitting of her wits last night against the threat of murder. The patience needed to teach those inattentive children, and the necessity to curb Willy's tongue . . . For the first time in her life, she feared the tasks she set herself to be too great. She longed to rest her head on Richard's shoulder and think of nothing more than the joy of being with him.

"When we are married," she said softly to herself. "When we are married . . ."

A log fell in the fire, shattering her dream. She looked dazedly around the room. Like a shaft of brilliant sunlight piercing the mist of illusion, the reality of her words was borne in on her.

Stifling her usual good sense under the wonder of Richard's love, she had looked no farther to the future than the happiness of being his wife, never to leave him. But to be the wife of Richard Carryll was to be mistress of the Manor with a staff of servants under her, to ride in his carriage with a footman running to place the steps for her to alight; a groom to hold her horse. She saw herself, sitting primly with a little cap on her unruly curls, in the Manor drawing-room, presiding over the tea-table, and amongst her guests—Arabella Glynde! Back into that haughty girl's teeth she would fling the remark about bad manners. But no; it would be more dignified to ignore it. She would conduct herself, for Richard's sake, as well as any high-born lady.

Then that dream also faded. For she knew that neither Miss Glynde, nor any other of the quality, would visit a house whose mistress was not of their class.

Well, what did she want with tea-parties and polite foolish conversation? Richard had never entertained. Was it likely he would change his habits? If she proved an embarrassment to any unexpected guests, she had but to make an excuse to withdraw. Surely he would not think it of the least importance? They would live as they had done all their lives, enclosed in their own little world, cut off in this corner of Sussex from the necessity to mix with society. In time, when she gave him a son, he would want nothing more.

Shrugging off the doubts which still lingered in her mind, she took up the candles and went with Judith into her front parlour. Above the clicking of knitting needles, her voice took on the low, rich tone which gave the words of Shakespeare all their beauty.

After a while she became aware of a draught upon her neck. The door to the back parlour was open. Propped against the jamb stood Jamie, head on one side, his gaunt face softened by candle-light, his eyes no longer suspicious.

Kate held out her hand. "Come to the fire. Or will your mother punish you if you do not go home?"

Ignoring her question, he limped to her chair. Tentatively, he touched with one finger the book she held, and looked into her face.

"Those words—they are in the book?"

"What words, child?"

131

"The words you spoke."

"Yes. They are written here. See." She held up the leather-bound volume which had been a gift from Richard, and pointed to the printed lines.

"Those little black marks are what you spoke? How can you tell?"

"By knowing your alphabet, and thereby being able to read."

"You teach the children that—to make those good words come off the page into your mouth?"

She stared at him. "Yes, Jamie," she said on a note of wonder. "That is just what I do. But—"

Lulled by the enclosed quiet of the room into an unfamiliar sense of safety, he ventured, "That's why I stand beside your window, mistress. 'Tis not to pry."

"You come to listen—to what I teach?"

He nodded. "Not the figures. I can count—enough to know my coins. But the reading out of books, and the stories of other lands—"

She visualised her schoolroom, the fidgeting children on whose ears she felt half her words fell as upon stony ground. She recalled the reluctance with which they trailed inside each morning, the sudden galvanising into life when it was time to escape. Their parents paid hard-earned money for them to learn. But to most of them school was a form of punishment, forcing their limbs to inactivity when there were birds' nests to rob and tadpoles to be caught, eels to be lured from the muddy depths of the estuary.

But here was this boy, ragged, unkempt, his crutch held together by a tattered strand of rope. Knowing nothing of life save neglect and pain, he yet sought knowledge and beauty.

She turned away. The flames leaping from the logs wavered, ran together in a blur of yellow through the tears which filled her eyes. Not trusting her voice, she drew up a stool and motioned the boy to sit. Anxiously he looked from her to Judith.

"If my mother knew—"

Judith stretched out her hand, feeling for his sleeve.

"Do not be afraid. Kate will not let any harm come to you. She will protect you—will you not?"

Kate brushed the back of her hand across her eyes. "I will do my best," she said firmly. "Now, I will read to you both."

Judith's needles clicked softly. The fire crackled cheerfully save for an occasional hiss of protest as a drop of resin fell into its heart. The memory of the previous night's violence was dispelled by warm and gentle thoughts. Kate's voice vibrated, filled now with an emotion she had no need to simulate. The boy, chin on hand, moved not a muscle; nor did his eyes leave Kate's face. When at last she ceased reading, he sighed deeply, blinking as if he were waking from a wondrous dream.

In a croaky whisper, he pleaded, "Would you say the bit again, about the candles going out?"

Turning back the page, she repeated the passage. "You can learn that for yourself, Jamie. Say it after me. 'Night's candles are burnt out, and jocund day stands tiptoe on the misty mountain tops.' "

After three repetitions, he was word-perfect. He folded his arms about his thin body as if he were hugging a precious secret. For the first time, Kate saw him smile.

She bent forward, rested her hand gently against his cheek. Unconsciously it was the same gesture she had used towards Richard the first time they met.

"I will teach you to read, Jamie."

A shudder ran through him. Slowly he turned his head. She saw the dawning of an incredulous hope; followed immediately by the familiar suspicion and distrust.

She took his face between her hands and said again, "I will teach you—if you would like that."

Into his expressive eyes there came a look she had never aroused in a child before. Admiration, awe, laughter—they had all flitted across the faces of her pupils; gratitude and love were often on Judith's lips. But this was worship. She dropped her hands to his shoulders. She could no longer hold his gaze. For she knew herself to be looking in to the yearning soul held prisoner within his twisted, tortured body.

Suddenly he went rigid, listening. From across the street came the notes of his mother's bawdy song. He shrank against Kate's knee, his face ashen.

"Have no fear," she told him. "I will hide you. There is—"

She broke off. Above the drunken caterwauling, she had heard another sound. Judith dropped her knitting. Turning her head towards the door, she listened intently.

Horse's hooves thudded to a standstill outside. There was a creak of leather as a man dismounted; a flurry of hoofbeats and clinking iron as an animal was tethered. Then, twice upon the door, the rap of a riding whip.

Kate sprang to her feet, staring across the room. Judith stretched out a hand, seeking reassurance. Automatically, Kate grasped it, while she summoned her wits. The boy trembled so violently he shook her skirt.

"Go into the yard," she whispered. "Hide in the dairy. If this is—who I think—there will be questions. When it is safe for you to come out, Judith will fetch you, if—if I am not here."

He picked up his crutch. He hesitated, looking from her to the door. She pushed him towards the back parlour.

"Go, child. You have enough trouble without being involved in this."

The double rap sounded sharply again.

"Who is it?" Judith whispered. "You are anxious, Kate."

She pressed Judith's hand. "There is nothing to fear. Only, if it is a—a stranger, and he asks questions, you know nothing. You cannot see, and any strange sounds you hear at night are but part of your nightmares. You understand?"

Horrified, the girl breathed. "The—the Preventive men?"

"So I surmise."

Kate stood, unmoving, as if by holding off the moment of opening the door, she could withstand the process of the law. She had not thought to face it like this, alone, her loft full of contraband spirits, her mind a deep lake of compassion, slow to respond.

She summoned up self-derision to allay her fear. Fool that she had been, to trust that smooth-tongued, innocent-faced lackey of Sir Henry Glynde's. Saving his life because he had saved Judith's; listening, soft-hearted and simple-minded while he thought up his lies to deceive her—that unlikely tale of love for a blind girl he had seen but once. All that she could hope for now was that she might have the wits to ensure that her folly should not endanger anyone but herself.

Releasing Judith's hand, she braced her shoulders, threw up her head, and strode to the door. A hand on the latch, she prayed silently for courage.

Then she opened the door.

9

On the shadowed step stood a man in a long riding coat, cocked hat pulled low to hide his face. Without waiting for Kate to speak, he pushed past her, motioning her to shut the door behind him. Her protest was cut short as he raised his head.

"Richard! Lord save us, I thought you were an exciseman!"

Laughing with relief, she caught his hands. "I have been reading *Romeo and Juliet*, which you tell me is out of favour. Yet, are you not Romeo, coming to me secretly in the darkness?"

"I have not come to play the lover, Kate."

Astonished at his tone, she stared as he laid his hat and whip upon the settle. Then, as he faced her, she saw the anxiety on his face.

"Richard, what is it? Something has gone amiss?"

"Indeed it has," he muttered. Recollecting himself, he greeted Judith. The girl gathered up her knitting.

"You wish to speak to Kate alone? I am quite ready for bed."

Kate answered for him. "It is best, child. The less

you know, the better. I will come to you later."

She watched Judith to the head of the stairs. Then, remembering Jamie, she fetched the boy from the dairy and settled him in the back parlour.

"You have the sense not to listen at the door, I trust," she warned him. Dumbly he nodded, frightened back into his shell by the interruption of his dreams.

When she returned to Richard, he had taken off his heavy coat and was standing before the fire.

"Now, why are you here—since it is not for the reason which would please a woman's heart— But first, will you take some wine?"

He caught her wrist. "Kate, will you attend to me. This is no time for wine."

"Nevertheless, you would be the better for some," she remarked evenly, fetching a bottle of Madeira. "What dreadful news have you to give—that I am to expect the militia on my doorstep within the hour?"

Exasperated, he exclaimed, "Kate, you are incorrigible. Will you not listen to me?"

"Certainly, when you are seated in the chair with some wine down your throat." She handed him a glass. "I know you, Richard. I have no doubt that when you tell me what plagues you, we can settle the problem with little trouble."

Imperturbably she spread her skirts around her while he drained his glass at a gulp.

"Oh, that Jesse had been at the inn when I called!" he said.

"You have tried to speak with Jesse? Then it *is* serious! I'll not interrupt you again, I promise."

Leaning forward, hands clasped between his knees, he announced gravely, "Tomorrow morning the excisemen will come to the village—to examine the hollow tombs in the churchyard. Now, do you understand what danger we stand in?"

She sipped her wine, letting it trickle slowly down her throat while she savoured this news. Then, putting down her glass with deliberate calm, she threw back her head and laughed, rich and full.

Richard frowned. He had endured long hours of polite conversation at the Grange, while half his mind was set on escape, to give warning and carry out a plan to outwit the law. Now, his anxiety taunted by Kate's laughter, his patience snapped.

He slapped her hard across the cheek.

Her head jerked backward. She sprang to her feet, hands clenched, eyes darkening, the colour flaming from neck to brow. Speechless with dismay at his own action, Richard rose also.

Kate put a hand to her burning cheek. For a long moment they stared at each other, neither speaking. Then, her body relaxing, she looked at him from under her lashes. He was utterly confounded to see that she was smiling.

When she spoke, her voice was low, holding the warmth that was ever his undoing.

"It seems you are more of a man than I thought. Now, you will doubtless know how best to atone."

With an almost imperceptible movement, she turned her cheek towards him, swayed her body forward. He touched the burning spot with his lips. Then, since he was adrift in a sea of uncertainty and she was a warm and comforting haven, he held her close and hid his face against her neck. Her heart nigh to bursting to have him so close again, she stroked his hair, murmuring reassurance.

"See, I was right after all. There is no need for anxiety. You plagued yourself to no purpose."

"But, Kate—"

She held him still, pouring out her strength like water from a deep, unfailing well.

"They will find nothing in the churchyard—the Preventive men. The kegs are no longer there."

He jerked away from her. "Not there? Where, then?"

Smiling, she pointed. "Above, in my loft."

"Kate!" The word held exasperation and despair. "You promised me you would not hide contraband goods here any more."

"I meant to keep that promise. But—this was an emergency. I knew you would disapprove, and we had little time. So—"

"Why did you move those kegs? Have you had warning also?"

"Not warning. Suspicion, rather, that this might happen. The church was honoured by a visit—from a certain lady—"

He broke in, "Are you sure that they cannot be traced here?"

She recalled the previous night's events, the appearance of Jonathan which had filled them with alarm; her decision which had averted a murder in this room, and the doubts which had assailed her afterwards. She was on the point of telling Richard what had happened. But, studying his face, she saw the anxious crease between his brows, the patches of white at the corners of his mouth. She knew there was a limit to which his nerves could be stretched. Boldness to her was as natural as breathing. For him, courage was a virtue to be fought for against a thousand fears she never knew.

139

Calmly, she replied, "Quite sure. It was done with only two men, Jesse and the ostler from the inn. There was a gale, as you will remember, which drowned all other sounds. Even Judith was not aware of what went on." She laughed again. "The village will have a peepshow tomorrow. I wonder, will Sir Henry attend to witness the discomfiture of the representatives of the law."

"Since it is he who is responsible for their coming, I think it very likely."

Her eyes shone with merriment. "Indeed, then, I must shut school for an hour to enjoy the best entertainment we have had for years. Oh, I am glad, glad, that I may thrust that laugh back in his throat and sound it in my own. And strike a blow at that haughty creature, his daughter."

Puzzled, Richard started to question her. But she was off on another train of thought.

"Richard, how did you learn of this? Surely Sir Henry Glynde himself did not tell you?"

"Certainly not. He amuses himself with twisting my tail, hinting he has certain information, trying to trick me into an unwary word. No, it was from the excisemen themselves—at least, by their spokesman—"

She threw back her hand and let out a peal of laughter. Seeing his shocked expression, she caught his hand. "Oh, Richard, Richard, can you not enjoy the joke? Here is this erstwhile magistrate and his prying daughter, thinking to wipe out a hornets' nest of lawlessness within his first month in the district. And what happens? The first time the Preventive men are sent to trail us, they let themselves be taken without a fight and plead a fever so that they may not face Sir Henry for a space. And now,

140

when he thinks to administer a *coup de grâce*, they send us word of warning. Indeed, I think Sir Charles's ghost must be rocking the walls of Falcon Grange with his mirth."

Despite his unease, he could not resist the infection of her chuckles. She poured more wine and sat down again, drinking a toast to Sir Charles's memory.

"But still you have not told me—where you heard the news."

"You gave me scant chance. You are like a fey creature tonight, Kate. There is little sense in you."

She leaned forward to rest a hand on his knee. "The time for common sense was yesterday. Tonight is for happiness, since you are here. A woman in love must be allowed to let her feet skip off the ground at times. Is it not the same with you? Do not your spirits soar skywards, as the lark, with joy at thoughts of our marriage?"

He stood up, not looking at her. "Kate, you must not expect too much of me. I do not come to decisions as quickly as you. I—I must have time—"

She slid to her knees and held his hand against her cheek. She spoke gently, her eyes soft and dark.

"Think you I do not understand? You said you would not have me other than I am. But I would wish to be, Richard. It would be more becoming if I blushed and drew away from you, and led you a pretty dance so that you did not know whether I really cared or was but playing with your affections."

Unconsciously her words were to him the perfect description of Arabella. Every graceful movement, every seductive turn of her head, the faint mockery of her smile—were they but artifices to capture the heart of a man as innocent of feminine wiles as himself? Or was her charm completely natural, and she as innocent as himself in affairs of the heart? He wished to believe her so, and that the tenderness in her voice was for him alone, that the momentary show of will this morning had been but reaction to her fear in the woods.

He looked down at Kate's dark head, resting against his thigh. She was like quicksilver, running this way and that in her changes of mood, expecting him to follow at the crook of her little finger. If he married her, he would spend his life trying to follow her lead. Again he told himself she would dominate his life, his home, and that was not the way of happy marriage. The thoughts went round and round in his brain, like an exercise learned in the schoolroom. Together with the captivating image of Arabella, they blinded him utterly to the fact that Kate was kneeling at his feet, quiet and still, more vulnerable than she had ever been in her life, waiting for him only to show himself her master.

Sighing at his lack of response, she rose, releasing his hand.

"I' faith, my behaviour is totally unseemly—receiving you here alone, at night. It were far better that you paid court to Miss Glynde, who is so beautiful and elegant, and—and of your standing."

Seeing him flush, she said, "I am but teasing you. Though 'twould be as fascinating as a game of chess, as you checked her suspicions of your activities with a string of compliments."

She forced her thoughts back to earth. "It is she, of course, who is responsible for the tombs being searched."

"Arabella? What nonsense is this?"

"Indeed, it is not nonsense! I came upon her prying in the churchyard."

"But how is that possible? How could she, or indeed her father, suspect what lay hidden there?"

"That I do not know. But why else should she venture into the long grass under the sea wall, damping the skirt of her new riding habit? She had been to visit her uncle's grave, she said—and he buried near the gate, as she well knew."

"It would be natural for her to be curious about the—the resting place of her ancestors."

"Almost I could believe you championing her Richard." She studied his averted face. "You called her *Arabella*."

He shrugged in an attempt at nonchalance. "It is her name."

She said slowly, "Tom Blackmore's boy came late to school. He had been to Chichester, he said. Later I heard him tell the other children that by the town cross he had seen the new mistress of the Grange, with her groom. They had been joined by Mr. Carryll, he related. I had thought it a chance meeting. I was wrong?"

"I—I escorted Miss Glynde into Chichester. I had expected her father to accompany us, but he was occupied with his notary."

She stood in silence for a moment. Then she reflected, "You had the information from the excisemen, you said: In Chichester?"

Relieved at her apparent change of subject, he answered quickly, "From the innkeeper at the Crown. You know that often he acted as go-between."

"This morning?"

"About midday. Why do you ask?"

"You had this information at midday, and yet

you did not come with your warning until evening?"

He saw now where her questions were leading. He murmured, "I had been invited to dine at the Grange. By the time I could excuse myself, it was late."

"It never occurred to you to refuse the invitation?"

"How could I, at the last moment? It would have seemed the height of discourtesy."

"You mean—you did not wish to?"

Because his conscience had troubled him, and he had found that Kate had saved the situation while he had been dallying, he turned on her.

"Very well. I did not wish to."

Her eyes blazed. Her tone was bitter.

"It seems the freetraders place their faith on a frail rock. I surmise you were so enthralled by this —this creature's charms that you forgot all else."

She had spoken at a venture. Suddenly, studying his face, she saw her words were true.

"Richard, can you not see? She is but using you, on her father's instructions, to try to wheedle information out of you."

"You are scarcely flattering. Does it not occur to you that she may regard me—in another light?"

She drew back. For a long moment she looked at him. Then she said, in a low voice. "Yes, you are right. I have assumed too much. You are, in truth, the most eligible bachelor within many miles. Already she has spun her web for you."

The sarcasm in her tone was her undoing. Richard exclaimed angrily, "It is you who have done that, Kate. You are like a certain species of spider which, having drained him dry, kills her mate."

She stiffened, staring at him wide-eyed, a hand at her heart as if she had been struck. He stepped forward, horrified at his own words, seeking to make amends.

She flung on her heel. Crossing swiftly to the door, she flung it open.

"Go to her! Make a fool of her as you have of me, with your easy promises, your sudden embraces. But doubtless she is cleverer than I. She will have your ring on her finger before *she* reveals the secrets of her heart."

He stretched out his hands, pleading with her. "Kate, forgive me. I did not mean—It is just that —that you are so strong, and I—"

"You are weak—or believe yourself to be? That has always been true. I loved you none the less for knowing it. But will she? Or any other woman? They will see only the outward seeming weakness, while I—"

She finished the sentence only in her mind. While I have knowledge of the years when you were as lonely and unloved as Judith or Jamie, though you never starved for lack of food. She saw the child, crying, uncomforted, in the dark cavern of the Manor bedroom, bullied and harried, ignored by his father, his spirit all but crushed. Then the struggle for independence and the desperate, determined efforts to conquer fear. And in all this she had been with him. Yet she had failed, it seemed, since even now he believed himself less of a man than she knew him to be.

When she remained silent, he put on his coat, picked up his hat and whip. Once more he appealed to her. But she would not look at him. Her body rigid in the pose he knew so well, shoulders thrust

145

back and head high, she stared into the darkness of the street.

"Since I am no more to you than the crutch is to that boy yonder, you may cast me off as easily. You cannot court two women, Richard; nor can you exist in two camps. Since you have chosen that of the enemy, it is best you quit the freetraders. Only, the plans being already made for the next run, I pray you to direct it. After that, you may do as you will, and none of us will intrude on your life in any way—I, least of all."

At the catch in her voice, he laid a hand on her shoulder. But she was totally unresponsive, moving not a muscle.

"It grows cold here by the door," she said stiffly, "and your mare restive."

Helplessly he dropped his hand, put on his hat. Without a word, he went from her into the night and rode for hours, as he had walked that other night, and came no nearer than he had done then to knowing that with one simple action he could have settled all differences between them.

On the chair beside the fire lay the leather-bound volume of *Romeo and Juliet* which Richard had given Kate on her sixteenth birthday. She picked it up, still open at the page she had been quoting.

To find one day a child whose mind could be opened to the beauty of words as hers had been opened by Richard. Such had been her dream. How often she had longed for it, and been faced instead by the gabbling repetition in the schoolroom. Now she had found such a one, discovered the soul of a poet in a crippled ragamuffin. And in the same hour as her overwhelming humility and joy at this revelation, she had sent away in bitterness the man who would for ever hold her heart.

She opened the door to the back parlour. Jamie slept, head cradled on his arms upon the table. She stood, looking around the room, mentally moving through the rest of her home—the schoolroom where she earned her bread; the small dairy where she churned her own butter, the yard with the pump with the creaking handle, the little bedroom where Judith slept, and above, the kegs of spirits.

At Falcon Grange now, Arabella's maid would be hovering round her in the big bedroom, and for her mistress the morrow would bring no greater problem than how to dress her hair.

Some words once spoken by Sir Charles came into Kate's mind. "You hide a heart of gold beneath a will of iron. My niece Arabella conceals her steel behind the most charming and provocative manners. I do knot know which is the more troublesome to a man."

"But I know which will capture his heart," she told herself. "I have fooled myself too long."

The dream was over, and the foolish fancy that Richard would always want her. Here, under her own roof, were the two who had real need of her —to whom her strength was salvation and not a snare to be avoided.

She touched Jamie lightly on the shoulder, quickly reassuring him as he cowered away from her.

"Do not be afraid, child. Come with me, into the front parlour. It will be warmer there, in the night."

Drowsily he followed her and curled into her deep, winged chair. His eyes were full of dreams.

"Night's candles," he murmured. "Night's candles are burnt out—and—and—"

His head fell sideways as sleep overpowered memory.

"And jocund day," she took up the words. But beyond that she could not go. There would be no more jocund days, no more dawns which filled her with expectation and joy.

She took up her candle-snuffers and put out the candles, save the one to light her upstairs. Then, shoulders drooping, her feet dragging like an old woman's, she mounted to her bed.

10

Sir Henry Glynde stood before the fire, rubbing his thin hands together. The morning promised to be much to his taste. He had entered the village only to attend church and, insensitive though he was, he could not but be aware of the veiled hostility which greeted him. The villagers had been polite enough, bobbing curtsies, doffing their hats. He wished he could have provoked one of them to insolence, so that it would provide an excuse for clapping a man into the stocks.

When he came to this outlandish part of the country, he had expected to find the people completely out of hand under his brother's happy-go-lucky squirearchy, a den of wickedness into which he would bring the flaming sword of justice. He could not now wield the sword himself as he had in a London court with, he prided himself, great thorough-

148

ness. But he had made the acquaintance of the age-ing knight who ostensibly administered the law at Chichester, and realised at once that he himself could be the power behind the scenes.

A case of sheep-stealing, dealt with far too lenient-ly in Sir Henry's opinion, had been all the lawless-ness needing a magistrate's attention. There could be but one answer. Every man for miles around must be engaged in a crime more profitable, with the connivance, not only of his own brother, but that fool of a J.P. who admitted he could scarcely hear a word that was spoken in court.

Behind the villagers' deferential greetings and blank faces, they were laughing at him, he was sure. This morning he would show them who was mas-ter and that the law could not be treated with con-tempt. Within an hour he would have evidence of smuggling in his hands. After that, he would have every house in the village, every farm searched, and he would be behind those knaves of excisemen ev-ery step of the way.

He checked the time by his silver fob, and throw-ing a supercilious glance at his brother's portrait, went out into the spring morning.

In the drive he found Arabella already mounted, with Richard Carryll beside her. She looked at her father in surprise.

"Are you to accompany us, Papa? I understood you had urgent affairs to attend to this morning."

"That is true. I beg you to excuse me." He paused, his foot in the stirrup. "Unless you would care to come with me to the village. My business promises to provide some fair entertainment."

Richard said lightly, "You are fortunate, sir, if you can combine the two. May I inquire, what form this entertainment is to take. Since Sir Charles put an end to bear-baiting in the village, I cannot conceive—"

"It seems a more adventurous sport has been substituted, sir, that of law-baiting. Though I have no jurisdiction, here, I still uphold the law. Unlike the unfortunate bear, when provoked, *I* have the means to prevail."

Arabella sighed impatiently. "Papa, you talk in riddles. What is afoot this morning?"

Sir Henry, his eyes on Richard, answered, "I intend to exhume the dead."

"Papa! How shocking!"

Richard said calmly, "I do not comprehend, sir. Do you suspect some crime?"

"Certainly. But not of murder, as you may surmise. I believe there has been a violation of consecrated ground, that it has been used for other purposes than those for which it was intended. In short—the hiding of contraband goods."

Arabella flicked at her boot with a whip. "That subject again! Indeed, Papa, you are like a dog worrying a bone. I think you even dream of smuggling."

Sir Henry ignored his daughter. His pale eyes were still on Richard, who nonchalantly shrugged his shoulders.

"Your devotion to duty does you credit, sir. But I venture to suggest you are mistaken. I cannot conceive of our parson conniving at such vandalism."

"You are too innocent, Mr. Carryll. A parson is as fond of brandy as any man. He has but to hide his head on dark nights."

Arabella frowned. "I am becoming chilled, waiting here. Let us proceed, Mr. Carryll."

Her father narrowed his eyes. "Then you will not join me?"

"Indeed no, Papa. I have no desire to witness so grisly an affair, and Mr. Carryll, I apprehend—"

"Is entirely at your command, ma'am."

Sir Henry, glancing at the stable clock, gave them a perfunctory bow and set off at a canter down the drive. Richard turned to Arabella.

"You are of the same mind—that it would entertain you to visit the lake?"

"Indeed, yes. I have seen little of your estate."

"It is much smaller than your father's."

"But—you are not a poor man, Mr. Carryll?"

"No. When I come of age in a few months, I shall inherit a considerable sum."

"With no wife to help you spend it? For shame, sir!"

"You think I should marry?"

"Should not every man?"

"Sir Charles did not."

She laughed, accenting her dimples. "Oh, you should not quote my uncle, as an example. You have yourself remarked, he took his pleasures—unconventionally. I am persuaded you are not of the same stamp, but prefer the accepted code of behaviour."

He looked away from her, thinking of Kate. There had been no code of behaviour in their relationship. You could not bind Kate by conventional rules; she made her own, as her heart dictated. But he was not of her stature. He had been born and educated to a social pattern, and that pattern was one in which Arabella, with her breeding and background, fitted to perfection. Had not Kate herself said so last night? Last night . . .

The memory lay like a festering wound at his heart, for which he had no salve.

Arabella's voice held a hint of mockery. "You are solemn, sir. Have I put disturbing thoughts into your head?"

Impulsively he turned to her. "You have done so, from the very first moment I saw you—that evening in London, when the candle-light shone so softly on your shoulders, and the music made me—"

She tapped his knee lightly with her whip. "Mr. Carryll, my groom has sharp ears. You should choose your time for such remarks more aptly."

For a moment he feared he had offended her. Then he saw the teasing expression in her blue eyes. She murmured, "There is perhaps a seat, beside your lake?"

He felt a shiver run down his spine, and his cravat felt uncommonly tight. Studying him from under the brim of her hat, Arabella was amused, but faintly irritated. She was confident that she could win him within the hour if she set her mind to it, and yet . . . She wondered if she could so ensnare him that he would submit to being taught the foppishness of dress and manners which were the mode in her circle. She did not even know if he could dance tolerably. There was a great deal to learn about him. But it would help to pass these tedious months of mourning, when she must refuse even the invitation to such balls as were held in the dull houses of the neighbourhood. Many ladies in the country, she had been told, passed long hours gardening. She shuddered at the thought.

"You are feeling cold?" Richard inquired solicitously. "Shall we canter a little?"

"As far as the trees yonder? You have noted, I trust,

that I took your advice and ride a horse from my uncle's stable? I am assured this animal will remain unmoved by wild creatures in the woods."

He flushed at her reminder of the episode he had tried to forget. "I—I must beg your pardon, ma'am."

She raised her brows. "For what, pray?"

"For not coming to your aid yesterday, when—"

"You acted very properly, Mr. Carryll. For what purpose does one employ a groom if not to deal with such situations?"

He stared after her as she set off at a canter across the stretch of parkland.

"Other women will see only the outward seeming weakness," Kate had said. But Arabella had not seen it. Her attitude to him was still as he had longed for it to be, that of a weak and lonely girl towards her protector. If he could but continue in this light, so that she would regard him with admiring, adoring eyes . . . If he could only train himself to make quick decisions, perform some feat of daring before her astonished, marvelling gaze . . . Oh, then, what a world of magic might not lie beyond.

Kate, heavy-hearted after her quarrel with Richard, sighed with exasperation as Betsy Turner mumbled her hesitant way through the passage in her reader. The child, conscious of the boys' eyes on her, moved her head so that the sun, shining through the schoolroom window, made a halo of her shining ringlets.

"Do those words mean anything at all to you?" Kate interrupted.

Betsy's blue eyes widened in innocent affront. "Oh, yes, ma'am. But it is so difficult."

"It is difficult because you do not try hard

enough. You are not even faintly interested. Si[t]
down, while I say it over to you, so that you ma[y]
know how it should sound."

Into her mind came the awed voice of the crip[-]
pled boy. "You teach the children to make those
good words come off the page into your mouth?"

She sighed again as she started to read. Only a
few hours ago, life had seemed so good. Richard had
come to her, and she had found a child eager to
receive the knowledge and beauty she had to offer.
She had sent Richard from her in anger; and when
she came downstairs at first light, Jamie had disappeared. She supposed that fear of his mother was
still the dominant emotion in his life. And now,
here was this pampered, simpering creature, mur-
dering a poet's words, while at this moment Jamie
might be . . .

Above the sound of her own voice, she heard the
tapping of his crutch. Glancing through the window, she stopped in mid-sentence. The boy, bent almost double under the load of wood, hobbled awkwardly along the street. At the end of the alley
leading to his home stood the slut who was his mother, dirty of skin and clothes, stick in hand.

Eyes blazing, Kate flung down her book. Telling
the children to continue with their reading, she
strode from the schoolroom, caught up her cloak
and purse, and followed Jamie down the alley. By
the time she reached him, his mother had set about
the boy. The wood, so carefully bundled and tied,
lay scattered on the ground. Jamie's arms were
flung up to save his head from the savage beating.

Kate seized the woman's wrist, wrenched away
the stick.

"A word with you, mistress, I pray," she said evenly, though her hand itched to take up the stick and belabour this slatternly creature until she cried for mercy. But that would not help her purpose. Ignoring the foul language that came from the ugly mouth, she went on, "It would appear you have little affection for your son."

"Why should I? He was fathered on me by a master merchant in 'is cups. 'E died of the effort next day." Her cackle was echoed by a neighbour standing in her doorway.

Kate clenched her hands and strove to keep her voice under control. "Then he is of no use to you?"

"Like that wench you took in, he can beg, though I've to beat 'im to get 'im on the street."

"What value do you place upon him?"

"*Value?*" She spat contemptuously. " 'E's of no value."

Kate opened her purse. "Then, if I were to offer you a guinea for him, that would be generous."

The woman's eyes narrowed to slits while her mouth hung open. Her dirty fingers were already outstretched towards the money, when a crafty look came into her face.

"If so be 'e's of use to you, mistress, 'e'll be worth more than a guinea. The old Squire gave 'im more than that in a month."

"But the old Squire is dead, and you'll not get that amount from the new one. I'll raise it to two."

She heard the murmurs of the women behind her, closing in to enjoy this diversion. Jamie crouched against the wall, staring from one to the other, while his life was bargained for. His mother's besotted eyes ranged over the group. Insolently she fingered Kate's cloak.

"I'm a poor woman, Mistress Hardham. I've not

155

your learning to 'elp me earn good money. Nor are the men who call on me at night, of the gentry, as with you—"

Kate gasped. Involuntarily she raised her hand. She was aware of the stunned silence behind her, of the burning of her cheeks, the ugly triumph in the woman's eyes. Summoning all her self-control, she dropped her hand, took more coins from her purse.

"I will give you five guineas, and that is the end of it," she said quietly.

She turned to the encircling women. "You are all witnesses to this transaction. I have this day bought Jamie. His mother has no further claim on him. You are agreed on this?"

They nodded, astonishment in their faces. Yet by now, they would agree amongst themselves when she was gone, nothing that Mistress Hardham did should surprise them any longer.

The boy's mother counted the coins, gloating as she held them up to the sunlight. Then, cackling to herself, she shambled off towards the inn.

Ignoring the staring women, Kate put a hand on Jamie's shoulder.

"Come, child, you belong to me now. My pupils will be having their bread and milk in a few minutes. No doubt we shall find a bowl for you."

Unable fully to comprehend what had happened, obediently he went with her to the cottage. At the door she stopped, listening. She urged the boy inside and gave swift instructions to the widow who came each day to work for her. Leaving Judith in charge of the schoolroom, she put on her hat and went out again.

When the little cavalcade, whose approach she

had heard, reached the churchyard, she was standing beyond the sea wall, innocently watching the boats in the estuary.

A mildly protesting parson trotted along the path in front of Sir Henry Glynde. The two excisemen stared at their boots as they followed, looking as if they wished themselves miles away. The women, lured by the promise of further entertainment, moved nearer.

As the news spread, the whole village seemed to emerge from cottage and alley, to stand loitering round the churchyard. A few of the men shuffled their feet anxiously. But many years in the Trade had taught them to hide their feelings. Jesse Turner, standing with thumbs in his breeches belt, winked broadly at Kate above the heads of the excisemen. Her answering smile changed to a frown as she caught sight, behind Jesse's bulk, of the gangling body and tow hair of Willy who, without an excuse, had failed to attend school that morning.

The operation did not take long. Sir Henry rubbed his hands together while the Preventive men lifted the slabs of marble from the hollow tombs. The baronet, confident of his triumph, did not even glance inside. Instead, he faced the villagers, so that he could mark the guilty by their reactions.

But the closed, blank expressions betrayed no emotion. On the face of the burly innkeeper there was the suspicion of amusement. Suddenly aware of the silence behind him, Sir Henry swung round. The excisemen, shamefaced, silently shook their heads. The parson looked as though he would like to say, "I told you so."

Sir Henry strode to the tombs, peered inside. The parson covered his ears against the venomous hissing of the Squire's oaths. The slabs were replaced. The Preventive men exchanged surreptitious grins. Sir Henry, tight-lipped, his knucklebones stretching the parchment-like skin as he gripped his riding whip, walked to the gate. His steps were light, his body taut, as menacing as a cat stalking a bird. His cold eyes surveyed the silent group of villagers.

Unhurriedly Jesse removed his thumbs from his belt and stepped aside to let the Squire pass. There was a yelp as the innkeeper trod on Willy, hiding behind him. Sir Henry paused, pointed with a long thin finger.

"Hold that boy," he ordered.

The villagers appeared to be deaf, for none of them moved. It fell to his groom to dart forward and grab the escaping Willy. Dragging the boy by his coat collar, he hauled him before Sir Henry who, eyes narrowing, flicked the thong of his whip against his boot.

"You dare to make a fool of me," he said between clenched teeth. "I will teach you a lesson you will remember for the rest of your life."

The puzzled villagers made no move, except Jesse, who scratched his head and took a hesitant step forward.

Sir Henry raised his whip. The plaited thong streaked through the air, cracking like a rifle shot. The villagers gasped. Willy uttered a piercing scream.

Kate, landing in a heap as she scrambled over the sea wall, picked herself up and rushed down the path.

"No! No!" She flung herself between the baronet and the cowering Willy.

Sir Henry lowered his whip. "And who, pray, are you—to gainsay me?"

She bobbed a curtsy which was in effect a mockery.

"Katharine Hardham, sir. That boy is one of my pupils. I do not know what he has done to displease you. But I do assure you, he means no harm."

"Indeed? It was no more than a childish prank, perhaps, to lure me here so that the whole village should laugh at my expense?"

"If he came to you with some tale, sir, he had no intention— He imagines—" She broke off, disconcerted by those cold, pale eyes, seeking words which would save Willy and yet not give away any clues. "He is half-witted, sir," she added with relief. "It is impossible even to teach him—"

"I shall not find it so. Pray stand aside, that I may complete the lesson."

She stretched out her arms to bar him. "Sir, this boy is even now playing truant from school. I do promise you, if you will hand him over to me, I will punish him."

Sir Henry felt the eyes of the whole village upon him. He had two alternatives; to thrust this impertinent young woman aside and to thrash the boy, or to accede to her request. It was beneath his dignity, himself to remove her; to order his groom to lay hands on a woman of some standing in the village would be to court trouble. It seemed the lesser blow to his pride to withdraw.

He motioned to his servant to deliver the boy into Kate's hands. He moved closer and spoke almost into her ear.

"You have not heard the last of this affair, madam. I never forget, or forgive a deliberate affront."

Her dark eyes did not waver as she faced him, shoulders thrown back, head high.

"Nor I, deliberate cruelty," she answered firmly.

11

Kate smoothed the folds of Judith's yellow muslin gown and set a wide straw hat on the girl's head. A soft bow of silk ribbon lay against Judith's cheek, rounded now and healthily pink.

"You would suppose I am going to a ball," she laughed, "instead of for a walk in the woods."

"Who knows—you may meet your prince amongst the bluebells as well as at a ball."

Judith's face clouded. "To tease me about a prince is unkind of you, Kate. No man would love a blind girl."

"Would he not? Men do not have a set of rules for losing their hearts, child. A lovely face a pretty manner, can captivate them in a moment."

Judith was shocked by the bitterness in Kate's voice. But before she could inquire as to its cause, her arm was tucked into the older girl's and she found herself standing on the doorstep. She turned her face to the sky.

"I do not need you to tell me the sun is shining today. It has such warmth."

Kate squeezed her hand. "You are like a kitten. Come, let us go along the estuary path."

She hoped that nothing would prevent Jonathan from keeping this rendezvous of which Judith knew nothing. She had entrusted her message to Jamie, who was used to making himself scarce and had waited patiently near the outbuildings of Falcon Grange until such time as he could attract the young footman's attention. Then he had come hobbling back to the cottage and solemnly announced that Jonathan "would wait upon the ladies at the trysting-place."

Guiding Judith carefully over the tangle of tree roots and tidewrack, Kate feigned surprise when Jonathan's voice sounded close beside them. Judith gave a start, and pressed close to Kate.

"You have no need to fear this young man," Kate assured her. "It was he who saved you from the horses' hooves."

Warm colour flooded into Judith's face. Eagerly she turned her head, smiling shyly as she held out her hand. Jonathan held it a moment and then, with a gesture Kate found infinitely touching, raised it to his lips and bowed as deep as any gallant.

"I—I hoped I would meet you again, Mistress Judith. I trust you did not suffer any ill effect from your fright that day."

"I had almost forgot it—save for your courage, that is. I had no chance to thank you properly. I —I do so now."

It was he who coloured then, up to his ears. He put a hand in his pocket, fidgeting with some article he had hidden there, and looked hopefully at Kate.

Smiling, she disengaged herself from Judith's arm.

"Master Jonathan, I think Judith would feel safer with your support, along this treacherous stretch of ground."

The blind girl made a little deprecating gesture. But her face filled with delight as her arm was

161

tucked into Jonathan's, and he led her along the rough path. Once she stumbled. Immediately his arm went round her waist, and there it stayed, comforting, taking no liberties. Kate dropped a step or two behind, speaking once or twice to assure Judith she was not completely alone with a strange young man, however safe she might feel with him.

They halted beside a fallen tree trunk. Jonathan spread his coat for them to sit on. After a few minutes, Kate rose.

"I am going a few paces into the wood, to seek for bluebells. Do you stay here in the sun, Judith. I shall not be far away."

Jonathan threw her a grateful look. She saw him reach again into his pocket as she left them.

Automatically she plucked a bunch of wild hyacinths, breathing in their fragrance. But all beauty now held a piercing pain. She had contrived for Jonathan to meet his sweetheart. It was spring, and the world full of lovers. And Richard? At this moment was he gazing enraptured into the blue eyes of Arabella Glynde?

The flowers were suddenly intolerable to her, with the same intense blue as the eyes of her rival. She flung them down and started back towards the couple sitting upon the log. But one glance halted her, and she turned away, as she had turned from the revelation of Jamie's soul, knowing there were feelings too deep for the world to see.

Jonathan flexed open Judith's fingers, and gently pressed into her palm a slip of wood, some twelve inches long.

"I fashioned this for you," he murmured. "I know you cannot see it, but it is—"

"No. Pray do not tell me. Let me feel." Already

162

her sensitive fingers were moving over the surface. "It is rounded at one end, and—and carved all over. Here is a circle, and here a diamond shape and here—" Repeatedly her forefinger traced the delicate patterns on the polished sycamore. But she could not bring herself to say what she had discovered.

"Tell me," Jonathan urged. "If I have done it well enough, you should know what you are feeling now."

She took her hand from the wood and held it clenched against her breast. What her fingers had recognised was echoed by this strange, exquisite stirring beneath her bodice.

Jonathan bent his head and whispered, close against her hair. "Say it. Say it, Judith."

Her fingers again sought the intricate tracing.

"I think," she murmured, her voice trembling. "I think it is a heart, and inside are two capital letters. They seem like—like two 'Js.'"

"That is just what they are," he exclaimed, delighted. "For Judith and Jonathan." Moved by the ingenuous pleasure in her face, he went on quickly, "I am only a poor fellow, just a second footman. But I can read and write, and when my uncle dies, there is no other to whom he can leave his mercer's shop. He wanted me to—to prove myself first, to work for another master and learn the ways of the quality. But he is becoming old and frail; soon I think he will send for me to help him. One day, I shall be my own master and not beholden to a man like Sir Henry Glynde for my meat and bed. Yet, if I had not been his servant, I should not have met you."

"Why—why do you tell me all this?" she asked softly.

"Can you not guess? Because, having once seen

163

you, no other girl will make so much as a dent in my heart. It is wholly yours, Judith, and ever will be."

She turned a radiant face, full of wonder, towards him. The whole of her being sought to burst through the barriers of darkness. He kissed her hands and then, very gently, her cheek.

The clock in the church tower boomed its notes through the wood. Jonathan drew back, frowning.

"I must go. Miss Arabella ordered the carriage. If I am a moment late, she will—"

"She will not punish you, surely? I did but meet her once, but her voice was soft."

"Oh, she is kind enough. But she is her father's daughter, and the quality does not tolerate being kept waiting."

From somewhere out of her troubled past, she remembered a man's impatient voice shouting harsh orders. She shuddered.

"You are becoming chilled," Jonathan suggested. "I will call Mistress Hardham to take you home. I will ask her when we may meet again. It is not often I am able to leave the Grange. But I will find a way. For a few moments with you, I would gladly risk my life."

She stretched out her hand. "Oh, no, you must not do that. If—if you truly wish to meet me again—"

"You know that I do. But, though it fills my heart with sadness, I must leave you now."

Again he put her fingers to his lips before he turned away. Kate met him at the edge of the wood.

"I kept my word, as you did yours, Master Jonathan."

"For which I thank you, mistress. You still wish me not to come to the village?"

"It is better not. The man who threatened you is of uncertain temper. I cannot guarantee your safety if you should be seen again near my cottage."

"Then—you will send me word by the lame boy?"

"I will try." She gave him a searching look. "But I must be sure of one thing. That you do not harm Judith, by word or deed."

He stood, head high and eyes unflinching before her intense gaze. "I swear a solemn oath that I would die before that should happen."

He turned and ran along the path through the spinney. He had gone but a few yards when he stopped and hurried back to her.

"Mistress Hardham, I—I saw nothing in your cottage that night. But there is something I could tell you which perhaps would be of interest—or help —to you."

A little suspicious, she asked, "What is it?"

"My master has a sharp nose. On the day we first came to the Grange he sent me to ferret in a cave beneath a hanger in the park."

Sharply she drew in her breath. "So? What did you find?"

"Why, nothing, mistress. But if so be it should help you—to be warned—"

He broke off in confusion.

"You have done well to speak of this," Kate answered. "The other night I held your life in my hands. I surmise you are aware you could do me great harm, if—"

"That I'd never do. Rather, mistress, I'd seek to serve you."

She watched until his slim figure disappeared be-

165

yond the trees. At the edge of the path the blue-bells lay scattered and forlorn. Sighing, she gathered them up again, since she could no longer bear the thought of their wilting, destroyed by her hand.

Judith still sat upon the tree trunk, fingering the slip of wood, a rapturous expression upon her face. At the sound of Kate's step, she made as if to cover her gift. Then, like a child, she had to share her pleasure.

Kate turned the wood over, noting the care with which it had been carved and polished.

"Why, 'tis a stay busk, to put into your bodice. Did you know?"

"I—I had not guessed its purpose," Judith murmured, a soft flush creeping up her neck.

Kate folded the girl's finger's over her keepsake. "But you knew its purport? That it is meant as a love token?"

"I—I think this is a dream that must end in a moment. You had best pinch me."

Her squeak as Kate obligingly did so set them both laughing. But Judith fell immediately silent, wrapt in her dreams. Now into her life had come another being, another love. By her own hand, Kate was loosening the knot which bound this girl solely to herself.

A single curlew flew low over the sluggish water of the estuary. It rose until its beak was but a pencilled curve against the reddening sky, its note a haunting, lonely echo from beyond the woods, transcending the joyous calls of mating birds which filled the spinney. And in that moment, Kate knew herself one with the solitary bird, faced with an emptiness as vast as the sky.

The evening sun slanted across the estuary, laying its soft light upon the village, silhouetting the church tower into a square black wedge against the fiery sky. Around the boats, resting at grotesque angles upon the mudflats, scurried little groups of dunlin and bobbing redshank.

Kate sat on the old bench by the sea wall, gazing unseeing at the familiar scene. She had left Judith contentedly weaving, her face full of dreams, while Jamie's head was bent in deep concentration as he made his first attempt at copying the letters of the alphabet. She had closed the door upon their preoccupation, wishing to be alone with her thoughts in the quiet of the evening.

She sensed the latent pulse of the village beneath its apparent calm—the mounting tension which at midnight would be released into action. High water, and the moon half-hidden; the jingle of harness and thud of hooves; lanterns winking, and the ripple of water as the boats put out; and at last the long file of ponies beneath the dark tunnel of the elms.

But she experienced none of her usual reactions to the thought; no tingling up her spine or pricking of her scalp. Only the knowledge that the night would bring the first meeting with Richard since their quarrel, held any meaning for her. She would wait for him, as always on a run, in men's clothes astride a horse, and spend the next two hours encouraging, taunting him into action and decisions against which she sensed his being was in revolt.

Was it any wonder he had turned from her to the elegant, totally feminine Arabella? For herself, she knew now, the wisdom of love had come too late. Too long she had quenched the instinct which

167

bade her play the weaker sex. When at last she had longed for him to take the lead, her domination had proved too great; his submission to her will too ingrained a habit to break, even at the onset of passion.

If she had drawn away from him on that first evening, dissembled, played hard-to-catch instead of revealing her heart, would it have ended differently?

Ended? All the years of close and dear comradeship, of trust and loyalty, sympathy and affection —to be snuffed out like a candle in a moment of bitterness?

What had her life become these last few weeks, save a succession of violent quarrels? True, she had saved Jonathan from being murdered; rescued Jamie from a life of untold misery; substituted as Willy's punishment the lash of words for that of a riding whip.

But even here, in the peace of the evening, the churchyard at her back held memories of the clash between herself and Sir Henry Glynde, and that other exchange of heated words with his daughter. She realised now that her suspicions had been unfounded. Willy had been responsible for the information about the goods hidden in the hollow tombs, not Arabella.

Suddenly Kate knew what she must do. If she and Richard were to part, it must not be like this. If her pride and her too-strong will had driven him into the arms of another woman, then, though her heart should break, there should be no bitterness in her. She would go to him now, while the impulse was strong within her. She would beg him, in all humility, to forgive her for damning Arabella out of hand; release him from that foolish vow of child-hood and wish him well. Beyond that moment, she would not think.

She hurried along the paths she had trodden since childhood. In the Manor drive it was impossible to believe anything had changed. Richard's mare trotted across the meadow to take her offering of grass. The western windows glinted in the last rays of the sun as the house settled into the approaching dusk, filling her as always with the sense of harmony between the grey stone and the woods behind.

Fondling the mare, Kate let her eye wander over every well-loved detail, every gable, every window, the flower-filled border below the terrace, over the lawn towards the ilex-hidden lake.

This she had thought to be her future home. Here she would have found complete fulfilment, given Richard all the love now imprisoned in her passionate heart; brought up her children, cared for Judith, found a niche even for Jamie.

Such foolish dreams! And yet . . . Was it even now too late? Could she not, by the very force of her love, win Richard back? Was she, who had never accepted defeat, to be so easily thwarted in this, the most important crisis in her life?

Straightening her shoulders, she continued up the drive and entered the house by the side door she had used all her life. Once inside, memories flooded her mind—of the first day she had come, her first meeting with Richard. She had touched his cheek then, gently, with sympathy and quick understanding. If she were now to show him only that side of herself, if she were to be tender and suppliant, making no demands—surely he would not again close the door to happiness so cruelly in her face.

She paused, silently praying for the right words, for the power to subdue her hasty temper, to know instinctively how to act in this meeting which would decide her life.

Her hands already outstretched, her eyes dark and pleading in the shadowed softness of her face, she started across the hall towards the library.

The door to the drawing-room opened. She heard Richard's voice, a girl's rippling laughter. Too stunned to move, even to think, Kate stood, open-mouthed. Then, galvanized into action by the sight of Arabella, she glanced quickly round. From out of the memories of childhood, the means of hiding herself came to mind.

Swiftly, silently, she slipped into the alcove beneath the curve of the stairs.

Some half-hour previously, Arabella had exclaimed, "Papa, can you not let the subject rest? I cannot conceive that Mr. Carryll invited us to dine for the sole purpose of listening to a discourse on the iniquities of smuggling."

Sir Henry's lips tightened. "You are impertinent. And on the contrary, I find Mr. Carryll's interest keenly aroused each time I mention the subject. I am not yet persuaded, however, whether he favours the side of the law or the offenders."

"Oh, as to that," Richard shrugged, "I consider it of no consequence to myself. That is perhaps reprehensible in your opinion. But in this part of the country, as you may have discovered, sir, it is customary to adopt the attitude of 'live and let live.' I surmise it was otherwise in London."

"Indeed, sir, I pride myself that in my own district at least, the law was administered most correctly. Here, as you have remarked, it is regrettably not so. When a magistrate is failing in years and health as is Sir Thomas—"

Startled, Richard broke in, "You have met him?"

Sir Henry frowned at the interruption. "Although he did not afford me the courtesy of a call, I considered it my duty to make his acquaintance. That appears to cause you some surprise, Mr. Carryll. In fact, you seem quite disturbed by the news."

"You are mistaken, sir. I was but admiring your zealousness when you have so lately come amongst us."

The baronet paused in the act of taking snuff, suspecting sarcasm. But the young man's face was grave. Arabella, knowing her father too well to risk another indiscreet remark, stifled a yawn behind a slender hand, and glanced towards the spinet.

Intercepting her look, Richard bowed, inviting her to play.

He stood beside her, turning the pages of music, again aware of the seduction in her voice, fascinated by the caressing movements of her fingers on the keys. But his mind was working on another matter.

He had ridden that morning to Chichester, to ensure that the caves which would provide tonight's hiding-places were ready. He had been disturbed to find a lantern left upon a shelf, the half-burned candle and a tinder-box giving every evidence of recent use. He had hidden them in the darkest corner, resolving to impress once again upon the men the need for the utmost care.

Afterwards, from a ridge of downland, he had

noticed two horsemen riding down the lane to Chichester. Blinking in the sunlight after the gloom of the caves, he could not be sure of their identity. But one was dressed in black and looked uncommonly like Sir Henry Glynde.

Had he been merely out for exercise? Or had some hint, some careless remark, led him to the smugglers' cache? Now, following the baronet's disclosure that he had called upon a local magistrate, it seemed only too likely this was the case.

What then, of the plans for tonight? Dare they risk Chichester? Or would it not be wiser to continue further, as far as Horsham, even?

Richard cursed himself for a fool for inviting Arabella and her father on this day when he should have remembered a run was planned. He wanted to be alone, to plan and organise. Would it be for the last time, as Kate had suggested? Why not, since then he could pay court to Arabella with a clear conscience? He winced at the expression, remembering his empty words to Kate.

He became aware that the music had stopped. Arabella's eyes, puzzled and displeased, were on his face.

"I am sorry that I weary you," she remarked coolly.

Hurriedly he turned the page. "Forgive me. I was so lost in admiration—"

"Oh, no, sir, you were not. Your thoughts were far away, and I fear I have done nothing to lighten them. My ability, I own, is very poor—"

Contrite, he assured her warmly, "Indeed, you play with great feeling, Miss Glynde. I could but wish my instrument were more worthy of your skill."

She glanced at her father, rubbing his hands together in the gesture she found so irritating.

"You did offer, sir, to show me the rest of your portraits when the opportunity arose—"

Richard bowed and gave her his arm. Sir Henry, as before, declined Richard's invitation and sat apparently deep in thought as they left the drawing-room.

At the foot of the staircase, Richard paused. Arabella, her hand resting lightly upon his arm, inquired. "What has disturbed you, Mr. Carryll? You appear perplexed."

"I thought to hear my name spoken. But, since there is no one here, I must have been mistaken. Let us continue to the gallery."

Yet he could not give his whole attention to her idle chatter. The sense of Kate's presence had been too strong. It was an illusion, he told himself. She would not come to him, not after dismissing him with such scorn, such bitterness. Not for several hours would he have to face her, when she joined him under the trees at the beginning of the night's operations.

The thought of that meeting filled him with dismay. He stumbled on the last stair.

Arabella's tone was cool. "You still appear a little distrait, sir."

"Forgive me. There are certain matters which—"

"Are occupying your mind to the exclusion of—pleasure?"

"I—I fear so. But I will resolutely set them aside, and devote myself entirely to your entertainment."

Entertainment! Arabella echoed the word bitterly to herself. Walking in a draughty gallery, studying a collection of indifferent paintings! But if this were her only means of eventually returning to London, it must be endured. Her father's tolerance, even encouragement of her association with Richard Carryl had surprised her. Until today, when she had realised he had an ulterior motive, that the young man's words about smuggling were not to Sir Henry the joke they had been to her. It would appear he actually believed . . .

She glanced at Richard from under her lashes. Oh, it was impossible! Slim, elegant, quiet of voice and manner, he looked no more capable of leading a desperate band than her own father. She shrugged off the ludicrous idea and set her mind to capturing his attention.

"You would find the pleasures to be enjoyed in London a better distraction."

"I fear they would soon pall, ma'am."

She drew back in mock horror. "How can you pronounce such a verdict, when you have so little knowledge? Indeed, sir, were we in London now . . ."

Her next words were lost to him. For he had a vision of her as he first had seen her, surrounded by a group of fashionable gallants. Were they in London now . . . Was it conceivable that in the town she would give him a moment's attention?

He recalled that many times she had uttered her dislike of the country, her yearning to return to the capital. Could he really believe that she would be content to remain here, so far from her friends, her balls and parties and visits to the theatre—for love of him? But if not, why did she appear to enjoy his company, seek to allure him with her charms?

He heard Kate's words, providing the answer: "You are the most eligible bachelor within many miles. She will have your ring on her finger before *she* shows you the secrets of her heart."

He sighed as he remarked, "I hope you will find opportunity to return to London, Miss Glynde. Our pursuits are duller, perhaps, in your eyes. If you remain here, you will be as a pinioned bird far from its natural setting. That was how I felt in the city, so that I am able to understand—"

Arabella's eyes widened at the coolness of his tone. Somewhere, she realised, she had played her hand wrongly. She had thought that here in the gallery where before he had shown every sign of becoming ardent she would have him eating out of her hand. She had talked too much of London she decided; that had been indiscreet, when so obviously his interests lay around his home.

Swiftly, she sought for a change of subject; found her answer amongst the paintings above her head.

"That view, sir, must surely have been executed some years ago? It shows the lake without the group of dark bushes which now screen it from the house. In my opinion, it is vastly to be preferred in its former setting."

Unthinking, Richard made a quick response.

"It was Kate's notion to let the ilex grow so fully —to give the nesting swans and mallard some privacy."

Arabella dropped her hand from his arm. Her brows were arched.

"Kate? May I ask, pray, who is Kate?"

He realised with a shock that this girl asked as many questions and gave as little of herself away as her father.

"She is—my dearest friend," he said firmly.

"Indeed? And am I to have the honour of making her acquaintance, in due course?"

Stirred by sudden revolt against her cool, impersonal manner, he answered, "I understand you have already done so, madam. I believe you met Miss Hardham in—in the churchyard."

Arabella stepped back as if she had been struck. "*That* girl—your friend?"

He bowed, without answering.

"But—but you are a gentleman," she exclaimed, irritated into further indiscretion. "And Miss Hardham, I am informed, keeps the school in the village."

"That is so. She is an excellent teacher, and has a wide knowledge of the classics."

She stared at him. Gone from his face was any hint of ardour. Instead, she recognised a subtle barrier, and knew it to be of her own making. Bitterly she reflected that in London she had set her sights no lower than a duke. But now, if she lost this man, life would be arid indeed.

Desperately, she sought to win him back.

"You will remember, sir, I am new to the ways of the country. I—I have relied upon you to teach me —to show me where I am wrong. If I must learn a new code of behaviour, if one associates here with people who are not—not—"

"Not of your own class?"

She flushed, at a loss before the gravity of his gaze.

"There is no need for a new code, madam," he went on smoothly. "It is I who break the accepted one, and gladly. Since Miss Hardham does me the honour to favour me with her—her regard, I should be churlish indeed to reject it."

As he uttered the words, it was as if a clear, dazzling light shone into his mind, banishing all doubts, all anxieties.

He had yearned to play the gallant before Arabella. Instead, he found himself the champion of Kate, even if only in speech. Kate, who was mistress of every situation, who had no need of a protector, who . . .

He stared beyond Arabella, into the grey haze of the woods, seeing neither, but only a series of images. Of Kate, the night he had first taken her into his arms and a stranger tear had flickered like a jewel in the firelight; of her sitting, shoulders hunched, wounded by his praise of Arabella; of her wish that for his sake she had been born a lady. Above all, of her head resting against his thigh as she knelt at his feet, waiting—waiting for him to declare his love, to match her passion and fuse both into an overwhelming joy.

"Do not forbid me, Richard . . ."

When she had spoken those words, she had given him his chance. Fool, fool, to be so blind! To have fixed so firmly in his mind the illusion of her dominance, to be afraid of such love offered so freely.

What had he given her? A casual kiss, a few empty words. Was it any wonder that, sensing his rejection, she had loosed upon him that torrent of bitter words?

Unconsciously he whispered her name.

Arabella stiffened. Her eyes now were hard, her voice cold. "It seems, sir, you break *all* accepted codes—at this moment, the one of common courtesy. I pray you, be good enough to escort me to my father. It would appear our presence here both disturbs and wearies you."

Flushing, he attempted an apology. But already

177

she was hurrying along the gallery, her passage no longer a graceful glide, but swaying her skirt in uneven jerks. She did not speak to him again, save for a few conventional words at parting.

He watched the carriage disappear down his drive with a feeling of relief. Now he could be alone with his thoughts. His whole inclination was to go to Kate, to ask her forgiveness, to swear eternal devotion, to pour out into her understanding ear the doubts and anxieties which had beset him. Only, for the first time in his life, he could not do so, since those very doubts could only wound her. He did not know what he *could* say, save that Arabella was no more now to him than a transient dream, a phantom whose white finger had beckoned him into a world which was utterly alien.

His world was here, in his home and the village and the sharing of life with the people he knew and trusted—with Kate, who was his other self and ever would be.

He was about to call for his horse when memory halted him. There were more urgent matters to deal with than a lovers' quarrel. The plans for tonight must be altered. He must think, organise, allow for a longer journey since it would be folly to use the caves at Chichester. So far Sir Henry had drawn blank. But what information might he have, what plan hidden behind the white mask which served him for a face?

Richard tried to force his mind to the problem. But his thoughts proved truant. He walked down to the lake, thinking movement would aid concentration.

There was no answer there; only the cob swan to hiss at his intrusion.

Returning to the house, he went from room to room. But his whole being was an aching desire for Kate. Her presence, her voice, was everywhere. Only when he came to the drawing-room, did her image fade. Firmly he closed the door, upon the pale tints and fragile furniture, upon the spinet where Arabella had enchanted him with her provocative charms.

He strode across the hall. In the library, where he and Kate had spent so many hours, had talked and laughed and grown to be part of one another —there he would find courage and strength to face the unknown dangers which might threaten them all this night.

He stood before the fire, holding out his hands to the blaze, feeling the peace and warmth of the room envelop him. Soon now he would be with Kate. His heart thudded painfully at the thought. He closed his eyes, remembering how he had desired her, knowing that now there was no barrier in his mind against fulfilment; that they belonged to each other; that life would unfold for them together, as inevitably as the seasons followed one another in the woods, as the rise and fall of the tide in the estuary.

He flung himself into his worn, comfortable chair, stretched out his hand for the tinderbox. He touched, instead . . .

He sat upright, staring in unbelief. On the polished side-table was the gold cross he had given to Kate so many years ago. It lay, not in a tumbled heap as if flung down in anger, but the chain in a little mound surmounted by the cross. It had a pathetic air of submission, hopelessness.

With a shock, he remembered his illusion of hearing Kate's voice in the hall, his belief that she was near. She had been there, he knew now. She had come to him—seen him, heard him, with Arabella. She had come into this room of memories and laid down the trinket, gently upon the table, returning the pledge he had not fulfilled, humbly and alone.

With all the biting words he could muster, he cursed himself over and over, knowing the depths of self-reproach.

An hour later he rode down the drive, his plan still not complete. His mind was in a turmoil, out of which only one thought had any clarity—that in a few moments he would meet Kate, and that he must convince her, utterly and without leaving her any room for the slightest doubt, of his love, his desire, his utmost need of her. Words formed in his mind. He rehearsed them, his voice husky. But he knew that when the moment came, his heart would tell him what to say.

He frowned as the moon escaped for a moment from a mountain of cloud. The night was not dark enough. But the Frenchman had sent word and would even now be entering the estuary.

The cloud intervened again as he rode beneath the trees, making the darkness absolute. He heard the faint sound of a horse pawing the ground; the creak of saddle leather as the rider urged the animal forward.

He looped his reins over one arm, stretched out his hands.

"Katharine. My dearest Kate," he whispered.

But it was not her voice which answered. Silas, the shepherd, rode Tom Blackmore's mare.

12

Judith knelt upon the floor, her arms clamped like a vice around Kate's knees, her uplifted face twisted as if in pain.

"Kate, I implore you not to go. Three times now I have had this same dream."

"But you often have nightmares. They will pass, as your other fears have passed."

"This is no ordinary nightmare. Always the dream is the same—that you go out into the darkness alone, and I see you falling. Then there is a blank. But next you are stumbling along beneath trees, with your dress torn and your face bleeding, and then —you have gone, and I know you will not come back."

Impatiently Kate unlocked the clasp of the girl's fingers.

"You are being foolish. For one thing, when I go with the freetraders, I am by no means alone. For another, I do not wear a dress. Enough of this nonsense. It is time I changed my clothes."

But Judith would not be silenced. "I beg of you, if you love me—stay."

"You would have me play the coward because of some notions the gipsies put into your head? What would you have me tell the others—Richard, even? I cannot join you tonight because Judith has had a dream. It has no sense in it, but still it is an omen, and I must abide by it."

The blind girl cowered at the scorn in Kate's

voice, and buried her face in her hands. Relenting, Kate added more gently, "You will not be alone. There is Jamie now to sit with you. Will you not teach him some verses?" She turned to the boy, standing by the door. "You will keep Judith company?"

He nodded. "Is it dangerous, what you do?"

"The less you know about what I do, the better."

"I learned things, sleeping on a doorstep It was company, hearing the ponies going up the lane, and the men coming back afterwards, though I was afraid. I've known you were one of them all along."

"Then you must forget it, Jamie. If there should come a time when you are questioned—"

"I wouldn't tell. I'd plead deaf and daft afore that. You've been good to me. I wouldn't help put your neck in a noose."

A desperate cry came from between Judith's fingers. Kate stamped her foot. "That was a stupid thing to say, boy. Between the pair of you, you'd have me swoon with fear this night. I'll not listen to another word from either of you."

She marched into the back parlour and put a saucepan of soup to heat on the fire. Perhaps it would put some warmth and comfort into those two, and herself, before she went out into the cold night. In under the hour, when she had fetched Tom Blackmore's horse, she would meet Richard as usual under the avenue of trees. Her mind shrank from this meeting. What could they say to each other? Everything was over between them. For if he married Arabella, his life thereafter must be completely changed. He would leave the freetraders and end his association with herself. There was no alternative.

She laughed bitterly as she stirred the soup. Poor Richard! Escaping one woman, he had subjected himself to the silken snares of another. In no time at all, he would find himself in London, frittering his time away, spending hours on his dress and perfecting gallant speeches and all those little attentions which Arabella would demand. In London he would have no need of courage, unless he were provoked into a duel or set upon by a footpad.

She paused in her stirring. Once again she asked herself, had it been her own fault that she had lost him? Was her love, as he had hinted, too smothering an emotion for him to tolerate, sending him into the arms of the cool, impersonal Arabella?

Jamie appeared at the door, his face worried.

"Will you come, ma'am?"

"What is wrong?"

"Judith. She looks—unwell."

Hastily Kate removed the pan from the fire and went into the front parlour. Judith knelt on the floor, her face buried in a cushion. Her body was racked with shuddering sobs; she trembled so violently the chair rattled on the flagged floor.

Kate knelt beside her, tried to raise her. But the girl seemed filled with an unnatural strength to resist.

"Child, what is the matter? Are you ill?"

In spite of her questioning, she could get no answer from Judith. The girl's body was rigid in her arms. Jamie stared at them, leaning on his crutch, his eyes enormous in his anxious face.

Exasperated by the continued lack of response, Kate resorted to shaking Judith.

"How can I help you, if you do not tell me what is wrong?"

Judith's answer came at last in a broken whisper. "If you have any pity, do not leave me tonight."

"But why—because of this foolish dream?"

Judith raised her head. The pale lakes of her eyes seemed to focus on Kate's face.

"Because I am more frightened than I have ever been in my life."

"But I must go—I—"

Suddenly, staring from Judith to Jamie, she asked herself, "Why must I? What do I do that is so important? Collect a horse, lift a few kegs on to its back, lead it a few miles, unload, return it to its stables. No—more than that! I give Richard courage. Without me . . ."

The voice of honesty rose inside her. Without her, he was free. He had no more need of her. Instead, he had Arabella. Nor had those fifty men need of her. She had but played a game, revelling in acting the boy, imagining she was facing danger as her father before her had faced the challenge of the sea.

Richard had been right. Smuggling was not for a woman. There were other calls to answer, less adventurous but more fitting, here, under her own roof.

She pressed Judith's head against her breast, tightened her arm around the trembling shoulders.

"Hush now, child," she murmured. "Have no more fear. I will not leave you, ever again."

Too restless to retire to bed, after Jamie had returned from delivering her message at the inn and they had drunk their soup, Kate sat reading aloud. Every so often she paused as some slight, familiar sound disturbed the stillness of the night. Judith, calm now, was curled in the opposite chair. Jamie sat on a low stool at Kate's feet, stifling his yawns but resisting her suggestion that he should sleep.

184

She was only half concentrating on her book. Part of her mind was with Richard. She hoped that he would believe her message that Judith was unwell and could not be left; that he would not think she had deliberately failed him. But no, cowardice, physical or moral, was one trait of which he could never accuse her.

She wondered if the lugger had arrived on time, if even now they were unloading. Unable to sit still, she rose and added more wood to the fire. She stared at the window. Perhaps through a gap between the buildings opposite, she could catch a glimpse of the ship's lantern.

Moving the candelabra so that the light was screened, she opened the shutters a fraction and peered through. At first she could see nothing in the gloom. Then, beyond the glass, there appeared a round, dark shape, topped by a triangular one. A man stood outside, looking straight at her.

Heart racing, she tried to control her scattered wits. There sounded a faint tapping on the pane. A voice urged in a loud whisper, "Let me in. It's Jonathan. I bring urgent news."

In the darkness she could not confirm his identity. Pulling the shutters together, she glanced round the room. Above the chimney-piece hung a pistol of her father's. It was unprimed; but it looked fearsome enough. She reached for it.

Telling the other two to remain quiet and still, she strode to the door. Quietly she drew the bolts, raised the latch, and stood back.

Like a phantom, Jonathan slipped into the room. Startled, he raised his arms.

"I mean no harm, Mistress Hardham."

She laid down her weapon.

"I was not sure enough of your voice, or that you were alone. What brings you here at this hour?"

Judith had risen to her feet, pleasure and anxiety mingling in her face. But Jonathan's business was not with her. He was panting. His clothes were mud-spattered.

"Mistress Hardham, there is a light, far out in the estuary. Does that mean the smugglers are out tonight?"

Her dark brows came together. She exclaimed harshly, "You should not ask such questions."

"But—if they are, they are in great danger. I came to warn you—"

"What danger? Tell me, quickly."

"I could not sleep. I was at my window when I saw lanterns in the yard, and then Sir Henry mount and ride off down the drive. Then there was a strange sound, far off, a sort of thudding. I threw on my clothes and ran across the park." He swallowed hard, still striving for breath.

Kate shook his arm, as if he were a stupid child. "Well, what then?"

"Mistress Hardham, the militia are on their way."

The indrawn breaths gusted like a breeze around the little room. Quickly Kate recovered herself.

"How far will they have reached?"

"About a half-mile from the village. I cut across the park, scaled the railings and came straight to you."

She raised her hands to her burning face. "The men must be warned. So little time. Jonathan—"

"Only tell me where. I will go."

She looked at him through narrowed eyes. Her voice was hard. "How am I to know this is not a trick? That you have not been sent to betray us?"

186

Judith stumbled over the stool as she ran forward. "No, Kate, no. He would not do that. You must believe him."

He caught the girl in his arms and turned again to Kate, pleading with candid eyes for her to trust him.

"It seems I have no choice," she said at last. "You will find—" She broke off, a new thought flashing into her mind. "But they would not heed you—dressed as you are in the livery of Sir Henry Glynde. They would as lief murder you as listen to your words."

She turned swiftly, snatching up her cloak from its hook. "There is only one way. I must go, myself."

Judith's hand sought to detain her. "Kate, you promised."

"Be quiet, child. Think you I can remain here and let them all be caught—Richard amongst them?"

She flung open the door, calling over her shoulder, "I leave her with you, Jonathan. Comfort her, and my thanks be with you."

She sped along the narrow street, unmindful now of stealthiness, her chief care to avoid breaking her ankle on the hard, uneven surface. Impatient with the skirts which impeded her, she hitched them around her waist, holding them with elbows pressed into her sides.

Half-way around the inlet, she developed a stitch and was forced to pause, her breath coming in painful gasps. Far out over the smooth water, a ship's lantern rode serenely against the cloudy sky. She heard the familiar faint noises, the sudden jingle of harness, the creak of a rowlock. Then another sound, from behind the village, where the road to

Chichester cut through the fields. A rhythmical thudding.

Pressing a clenched fist into her side, she set off again. There seemed to be an echo to her footsteps, a strange, uneven echo. Imagination? Or was someone following her?

She stumbled, almost spent, into the reeds below the scrub oak. Raising her head, she uttered the call of the redshank, three times repeated, then again three times, and again, until she was sure the men could not have failed to understand her warning. Her heart seeming to be banging about inside her ribs, as she stared over the water, willing the telltale light to go out. Yet the moment when it was extinguished made her blink, hardly daring to believe she had succeeded.

She rose to her feet and continued along the inlet. Still the uneven footsteps sounded behind her. She had no time to investigate. She must get to Richard.

Too late, she saw the dark form emerge from under the trees. Arms pinioned, her mouth covered by a rough hand, she struggled violently against the man who held her. Then she was free. Silas' shocked voice exclaimed, "Lord's sake, it's Mistress Hardham."

"Take me to Mr. Carryll, quickly."

Aided by his hand beneath her arm, she ran the last few yards. The freetraders waited, silent and tense, by the water's edge. Kate hung on Richard's arm to support herself, striving for breath.

"The militia!" she gasped. "Listen! You can hear them."

In the stillness, she could sense the stiffening of bodies, the straining of ears. There was a muffled

oath. Then silence. She leaned against Richard, trying to regain sufficient strength to urge him to give
his orders.

But before she could speak again, he said quietly, "You all know what to do. We have rehearsed
this many times. Lay off with the boats at once. Silas, sending warning to the lugger to leave the estuary. The rest of you, disperse."

Even as she heard the tramp of marching feet growing ever nearer, Kate marvelled at the coolness of
Richard's voice. He added, with a laugh, "When
it is safe, you will hear a strange curlew calling."

An arm around her waist, he led her to where
his horse was tethered. Around them, the darkness
stirred with sudden, stealthy, movement as ponies
were mounted and ridden away and the loaded
boats put off.

An officer shouted an order. A shaft of moonlight
revealed the road to the village barred by a phalanx
of militiamen. A horseman left the group of soldiers,
galloped forward, drew his mount to a rearing standstill.

The voice of Sir Henry Glynde came out of the
darkness. "Stand, in the name of the law."

Richard leaned from his horse to lift Kate up behind him. Impeded by her skirt, she tripped and
fell against the animal's legs. Whinnying, it reared,
plunged forward. With Richard striving for control,
it bolted beneath the trees.

Sprawled upon the ground, Kate was aware at
first only of a searing pain in her ankle where the
horse had kicked her. Then she realised the danger
which threatened her from above.

"Richard, save me, save me," her cry rang out in
despair.

Sir Henry dismounted, shouting an order to the men behind him. She heard the click of a pistol hammer as he walked towards her. A pale gleam of moonlight escaped the enveloping clouds and fell full upon him. Beneath his black tricorne his face was a pale oval, his mouth a straight, unyielding line; his hand was unwavering on the pistol.

Cowering into the shadows, Kate was hypnotised into immobility by his relentless progress towards her. She heard again his laugh as on that first day when Judith risked death beneath his horses' feet. She recalled his words in the churchyard: "I never forget, or forgive, a deliberate affront." She knew she could expect no mercy.

He was within two feet of her when Jamie struck. Balancing himself on his one leg, the boy lifted his crutch. With the strength of desperation, he smashed it down upon Sir Henry's skull. Toppling over with the effort, he hopped quickly up and prepared for a second blow.

But it was not needed. Sir Henry Glynde lay still. In the moonlight, a dark pool spread around his head. His crushed hat lay a few inches away, the silver trimming faintly gleaming.

Kate struggled to her feet, wincing as she put her weight on her injured ankle.

"Jamie! Oh, child, what have you done?"

He dropped his crutch and flung himself, sobbing, into her arms.

"He was going to kill you," he choked. "I had to do it. Will I hang?"

Holding him close, she was aware of men running, of shouts and curses, and horrified faces encircling them. Rough hands wrenched the boy from her, pinioned her arms.

"Let him be," she pleaded. "He has done nothing."

"*Nothing?*" a man growled. "To kill a Justice of the Peace is *nothing*."

"It was not he. I killed this man."

A derisive laugh greeted her words. An officer moved forward.

"Your effort at self-sacrifice does you credit, ma'am. But we all have eyes, and the moon was most obliging at that moment. This lad is over-young to end up on a gibbet, and Sir Henry Glynde did not endear himself to me in the short time we were acquainted. But I have my duty to perform."

Vainly, against the restraining arms, she struggled to reach the boy who had signed his death warrant in a quixotic flash of courage beyond his years. They were binding his arms now, but his eyes, wide with appeal, never left her face.

The officer glanced around. "We came to capture smugglers. What know you of them, ma'am?"

In the horror of the last few minutes, she had forgotten why she was in this place. Now, even if she could not save Jamie, at least she could keep her wits about her not to betray the others.

"That they existed only in Sir Henry Glynde's imagination. He sent Preventive men to search in our churchyard and found nothing but two hollow tombs. He thought to find a cache in his own park and was discomfited to discover naught but an empty cave."

"What do you here then, ma'am, on so dark a night?"

"You ask an impertinent question, sir. Did you not hear a horseman ride away? And are you not aware that certain—gentlemen—do not wish their assignations bruited around the countryside?"

There was a chorus of ribald laughs which made her want to slap their faces. She clenched her teeth, praying that they might be content with her answer.

"And this boy?"

"He is my brother," she lied, avoiding Jamie's eyes.

The officer shrugged. "If the fish were here, they've escaped the net. We could search for hours, and men who know this country would lead us in circles and be back in their beds while we lost ourselves. It was a fool's game to think putting a block across a road would be sufficient." He looked down at the still figure lying at his feet. "Well, he's paid for playing the general, thinking he knew best. Bring up his horse. We'd best take him home, before he stiffens. You can sling the boy across, also, or he'll hold us back."

He turned to Kate. "And as for you, since your lover has left you to the protection of this one-legged devil's spawn you name as brother, you'll come too. You're lying. But I'll have the truth out of you, by one means or another."

Sick at heart, her spirit all but broken, she watched them lift the baronet's body on to his horse. They slung Jamie across the creature's rump, jamming his foot into the stirrup leather, while his arms dangled helplessly down the other side.

"Will you not even support his head?" she pleaded. "He is but a child in years, though his face has grown old with sorrow."

"So—we are to consider the comfort of this *child* who has just savagely killed a man?"

"He did it to save me. Can you not understand?"

The officer turned away, shrugging, and re-formed his men. They set off, Jamie's body jerking like a puppet's at every step of the horse.

"Is there not one among you with any pity?" she demanded, her voice near to breaking.

But they marched on in silence, their backs like ramrods, no longer men with separate hearts and minds. What was he to them, this boy they had seen only in that moment of his desperate bid to protect her? What did they know of the yearning for beauty which lay beneath, of the devotion which had made him follow her along the road to his undoing? She had taken him in, opened a door a fraction on a world he longed to enter, bargained with his mother for his hope of happiness, and now . . . Through her, his short spell of freedom was ended before it had begun.

"Night's candles are burnt out." Her throat ached as she whispered the words. So small a candle, so bright a flame, so soon to be snuffed out.

Richard, Richard, where are you? her heart cried. Why did you not come back to save us? You had fifty men at your command; yet you did not even try. You rode off, deserted me, when I so needed you. At the end, you failed. It was left to a mere boy to show you the meaning of courage, and of love. If you had ever loved me, even as a sister, you would have come back, called up the men to attack, and rescued us. Indeed, you are more fitted to hold the hand of Arabella and speak soft words of comfort upon the death of her father.

The jarring of her ankle on the uneven road added to her bitterness. She was dragged along, engulfed by darkness and pain, inside her an icy hollowness where before there had been glowing vitality. This, then, was the end of folly. Suddenly she knew it to be the end of hope.

For had not Judith described this very scene? "I see you falling . . . stumbling along beneath trees with your dress torn and your face bleeding." It had come to pass just as the blind girl had feared. And the rest of the dream? "You have gone, and I know you will not come back."

Somewhere in the darkness behind her, Richard was hiding, shrinking from decision since she was not there to give him strength. But as the stranger tears forced themselves from under her lids and trickled down her cheeks, they brought forgiveness. She could not censure him. Her love was total, encompassing the weakness she had always known and understood and believed she had helped him to conquer. Fail her in her hour of need he might have done. But he would hold her heart until the end of life.

13

Richard fell, spreadeagled, into a gully. His horse, at last free of the burden it had dragged along by one stirrup, crashed on through the trees.

After a few moments Richard made an effort to rise. But the force of his fall had winded him. He pressed his face into the damp earth and let the waves of nausea wash over him, drowning him in a blessed oblivion.

When at last he opened his eyes, they rested on some white object a few inches from his face. Blinking, like a man waking from a deadening sleep, he reached out a tentative finger. Cold, hard, smooth. A paperweight, perhaps? His fingers explored the surface on which the object lay. Earth, wet leaves, the empty cup of an acorn. He continued to identify without any significance. He realised the white object was only a stone. There were other stones, sharp-edged, pressing into his body.

He rolled over and sat up. After a few minutes his eyes grew accustomed to the darkness. A shaft of moonlight showed him the exposed roots of a holly bush, twisted into fantastic shapes. Fascinated, he continued his game of identification. A few scrub oaks topped the hollow. A litter of dead leaves and fresh earth betrayed a badger's sett. There was a curious sound coming through the wood, a rhythmical thumping, as if a giant were treading down the earth. He thought it must be his own heart.

He unfastened his waistcoat and put a hand inside his shirt. His fingers closed on Kate's gold cross. Memory, like a jagged flash of lightning, tore apart the veil of oblivion.

He scrambled to his feet.

The thumping noise continued, fainter now. He knew suddenly what it was—the tramping feet of the militia. There was no other sound, save the scrabblings of small nocturnal creatures.

Swearing as a root snapped in his hand, he clawed his way up the slippery bank. Faintly now, the moon shone through the trees.

He shook his head, trying to clear his brain and regain his sense of direction. Stumbling over tree roots, and silently cursing his horse which had bumped and battered him into this dazed state, he came at last to the road. He tripped over an object lying across his path. Stooping, he discovered it to be a crutch, roughly hewn. Jamie—*here?*

Richard called softly into the shadows. Receiving no reply, he bent again, searching for any clue which would tell him what had happened. His hand encountered something hard—a man's three-cornered cocked hat, black with silver trimmings.

He stood, holding the hat, desperately trying to free himself of the cloud of stupidity over his mind. Yet he sensed that this very inability to think properly was but a defence against the revelation of some nightmare truth he did not want to learn.

He walked a few steps, twirling the hat between his hands. Already, although he tried to shut out the knowledge, his mind had registered to whom the tricorne belonged. There had been a mounted man whose voice he knew only too well; and another voice, calling a desperate appeal.

"Richard! Save me! Save me!"

He hurled the hat from him, as if by that action he could thrust away the thoughts which now made of the silence a cold pulsating horror.

A whisper close beside him made him start.

"Mr. Carryll? I've caught your horse and tied it to a tree yonder."

"Who is that? Silas?"

"Yes."

"Where are the others?"

"Hiding in the woods beyond the inlet, I imagine, I stayed to give the signal, like you said. Everybody escaped save Mistress Hardham, and the boy."

"You mean, they—?" He could not form the words. "Tell me what happened. My horse bolted and threw me. I must have lost consciousness."

"I went down in the reeds, flashing the lantern,

when Sir Henry Glynde rode up. I heard Mistress Hardham call out and then, your horse it must have been, galloping away. I didn't see what happened. But Mistress Hardham called out, 'Jamie, what have you done?' When I thought 'twas safe, I poked my head through the reeds. Sir Henry was stretched on the ground. Two men had the boy fast, and Mistress Hardham too, and another held Jamie's crutch. 'Tis my belief he'd killed Sir Henry."

Richard closed his eyes. He had taken many a toss in the hunting field, but none had left him as dull-witted as this. All that filled his mind was self-reproach that he had bungled their escape and left a one-legged child to come to Kate's aid.

He became aware that Silas was repeating a question.

"What are your orders, Mr. Carryll? The men will be waiting, though they won't know—about the prisoners."

"They were marched off—with the militiamen?"

"Yes. At least Mistress Hardham was walking, though I think she was hurt. The boy was strung across Sir Henry's horse, beside the body."

"I—I must think, Silas. Leave me alone a space, and wait by my horse."

The silence of the night closed around him once more. He leaned his head against an ancient oak, praying for his mind to clear. The bark of the tree felt hard and rough under his hands. Through his fingertips he sensed the steady flow of sap, and he gripped the trunk more firmly, calmed by the tree's endurance.

A leaf brushed against his face. He lifted his head. It was as if Kate's hand had touched him. Clearly,

197

as if she had been there beside him, he heard her voice.

"You *can* do it, Richard. There is no fear you cannot conquer, no obstacle too difficult."

He said aloud, "If I have you, my Kate. God grant I am in time."

He strode to the edge of the wood, his nerves steady, his brain clear. By the time he mounted his horse, his plan was complete.

As fast as he dared on the rough track, he rode to the rising ground at the point of the inlet. Throwing back his head in a gesture reminiscent of Kate, he whistled the rallying call, the two-note ascending cry of the curlew.

It seemed an eternity before the men emerged from the trees and clustered silently around him. Swiftly he told them what had happened.

Shaking his fist, Jesse growled. "They'll not keep Mistress Kate while there's breath in my body. 'Twas she who came to warn us."

A chorus of assenting voices joined him, mingling with an oath or two.

Richard said crisply, "This is my plan. If any man sees fault with it, let him say so, but quickly."

When he had finished, there was silence for a space. Then Jesse said anxiously, "There's just one point, Mr. Carryll. Surely, they'll take Sir Henry straight to the Grange."

Richard exclaimed in annoyance. "You're right. It will have to be where the trees come down to the road below the main entrance to the Grange. We'll enter by the lower gate and cut across the park."

"And if the lower gate is locked?"

A man laughed at the edge of the group. "I've

not poached the Squire's deer for years without knowing more than one way into the park."

"Let us go, then. Remember, the rule remains. No bloodshed unless it cannot be avoided."

"It's up to them," Jesse muttered. "I'll blow the head off any man who lifts a finger against Mistress Kate."

As he wheeled his horse, the thought struck Richard, how Kate would revel in this manoeuvre. The reckless side of her nature would exult in this swift ride in the darkness, in the sense of comradeship of men bent on one purpose. Almost he could feel her arms around his waist, hear her laugh in his ear, as if it were some mad game they were playing.

Then his spirits sank. For her, it was no longer a game, nor an adventure. Somewhere beyond the village, she was a prisoner, a woman alone amongst a band of militiamen. Hurt, Silas had suggested. Perhaps imagining herself abandoned, left to fend as best she could while he fled to the arms of Arabella Glynde.

He pushed the thought from him, along with the possibility of failure. He must not fail. Though he be riddled with shot, somehow he must save her—and the boy, from the grim consequences of his heroic folly.

And afterwards? Only help me through this next hour, he prayed, help me to avoid bloodshed and yet retain my honour, and I will lay the world at her feet. She had given him her strength and her comfort, and the wild joyousness of life. He had given her—what? A knowledge of books.

He laughed contemptuously. Jesse, riding beside him, raised his eyebrows, thinking Mr. Carryll was belittling the task before them.

They skirted the silent village where the women-folk huddled together, hearing the tramp of marching feet, the pounding of many hooves, while they suffered the agony of ignorance.

The lower gate of the park was locked. Richard waited impatiently while a man dismounted and removed a section of iron palings. Part of Richard's brain registered the neatness with which the sawn metal fitted into place. He resolved to look to his own fencing, if . . .

On the short grass of the open parkland, they urged their mounts forward. They cantered out of the main gates in a bunch. On the road, Richard halted them.

"Jesse, you know the men's names better than I. Pair them off, twenty to each side of the road. For the rest you all know what to do."

Quietly each man took up his position in the invisible ambush under the black tunnel of the elms.

And now, temptation spoke to Richard in the gruff tones of the innkeeper.

"If you'd like me to call the soldiers to halt, Mr. Carryll—I've a sight bigger figure than you, a louder voice, too."

Richard hesitated. Was there not sense in what Jesse suggested? Perhaps he himself would be shot on sight, before his words could reach the officer. Yet, was not his own voice more likely to take effect—the tones of the "quality" which represented authority?

He drew himself up. "You doubt my ability?"

"No, sir, that I don't. Mistress Kate said once

that if you were put to it, you'd be the bravest among us."

The words were written in fire across the sky. He felt humbled by her faith in him. He had believed it false, this image of a man to whom she had offered herself, at whose feet she had knelt, vulnerable, suppliant. He knew now, with a burning clarity, why he had refused to kiss the cross he had given her, why he had sought refuge in the artificial charms of Arabella Glynde. It was not because he feared the domination of Kate's love, that her passionate nature would overwhelm him. It was because he had felt himself utterly unworthy of her.

This then, was his proving hour. If he survived this test and lived, he could claim her, with head high, his heart wholly hers, believing at last in himself as she had tried to teach him to do for so many years.

Muffled by the high hedges, the sounds of tramping feet, the jingle of accoutrement, approached from beyond the wood. Richard, emptying his mind of all thoughts save this one desperate purpose, tied a kerchief over his face and drew his pistol. In the stillness, every noise was magnified a hundredfold —a horse blowing through its nostrils, pawing the ground; a man's stifled curse; the sudden cawing of the rooks restless in their treetop nests.

He felt a quiver of nervousness run through his horse, and tightened his grip on the reins. The moon threw a fitful beam through the branches, exploring, seeking the night's secrets. Anxiously, Richard looked for any betraying movement under the avenue of elms. But the freetraders might have dissolved into tree-trunks for all that could be seen.

The marching feet came nearer. Round the bend

in the road came the militiamen, the white of their breeches and facings gleaming in the darkness. The moonbeam freed itself of cloud, wavered through the branches. Then, as if aiding the smugglers' plan, the clear light shone steadily, while into its pool of silver moved the column of men. In their midst a horse plodded along bearing two bodies bumping like rag dolls. And behind . . .

Richard caught his breath. Almost, at that moment, he was unmanned. But not from fear.

For the first time in their lives he saw Kate as a woman, helpless and defeated. With bowed head, and drooping shoulders, her dress torn and her face bleeding, she stumbled along the rough road. For her, the gay adventure was all but ended. All the warmth, the laughter, the compassion, would be ground out of her by the relentless process of the law. Like any common felon, she would be condemned, and . . .

Swallowing hard, Richard clenched his teeth against the intolerable desire to call her name, to rush straight to her side. All his fears, his anxieties, the dreaded numbness of brain, were overwhelmed by the great wave of love which invaded his whole being.

Calming his horse, stilling his own emotions, he calculated his distance. Then, head high, his pistol steady, his brain as cold and clear as ice, he rode forward.

The officer in charge of the militia rapped out the order to halt.

"What is the meaning of this?" he demanded.

"We require your prisoners."

The officer looked around him. "We? I see but one."

"My men are on each side of you, your retreat is covered. And I am here to bar your forward way."

"That I will soon alter."

The officer stepped forward, raised his arm.

The moment of Richard's hesitation was too long. The officer's gun flared. The report sent Richard's horse on to his haunches. He heard a whistling in his ear. The kerchief slipped from his face. His left cheek burned as though a live coal had been laid against it.

Kate's scream roused him to action. He raised his pistol, took careful aim, and fired.

The officer's weapon thumped on the ground. Clutching his right arm, he reeled backwards. He shouted an order.

Moonlight glinted on metal as the militiamen raised their arms. For one endless moment Richard faced the column of levelled muskets, alone.

A volley of shots from the trees blasted over the heads of the militiamen. A cocked cap was sent flying; its owner's musket clattered to the ground. The rest of the troop hesitated. Lowering their rifles, they peered into the darkness concealing they knew not how many men.

Richard rode forward.

"You have had your warning. There is a weapon pointed at every one of you. A volunteer's right is to die fighting, not to be shot down in cold blood. Hand over your prisoners."

The officer turned his back on Richard, looked down the line of his troop, hemmed into the narrow road. Swearing, he repeated his order to fire.

His sergeant's voice was loud in the tense silence.

"It's true, sir. We enlisted to fight invaders, not to march a dozen miles on a wild goose chase. What have we caught? A woman, a one-legged urchin, and a dead man. These fellows are welcome to 'em, say I."

"Your sergeant speaks sense," Richard urged.

"He speaks cowardice, God damn his soul. Do you think I'll surrender to you rabble without a fight?"

Please God you do, Richard prayed silently. Or I will have to order a holocaust of murdered and injured men. I, who swore to Sir Charles there never would be bloodshed.

"Captain—"

"Hold your tongue, you insolent braggart." The officer turned back to his men. "I'll have every one of you court-martialled who disobeys my orders."

"You cannot court-martial dead men, Captain. We shall take your prisoners. But not one of you will be alive, if you resist."

"He's right, sir," the sergeant urged again. "We haven't a chance. They can see us; we can't see them. The wood may be full of armed men."

Jesse's voice boomed out of the darkness. "It is. We'll have your wigs off in a trice."

Richard heard the muffled laughter, the impatient mutterings of his men; Matthew's voice, urging a second volley, aimed to kill.

Snatching a musket from the nearest man, the officer raised it in his left arm, faced his troop.

"I'll make an example—"

Richard leaned from his saddle. Grabbing the officer's epaulette, he sent him sprawling into the road. Sudden nausea making him sway in his stirrups, he strove for control of his voice.

"So much for your captain. Now you will obey

your sergeant, who has more sense. Sergeant, order your men to drop their arms."

He heard the shouted command, the cheers of his own band, the clatter of falling muskets. From a great distance Kate's voice came to him, calling his name. His left cheek burned; blood made a wet rag of his cravat. The world was dissolving in a whirling phantasy.

Brandy, all that brandy, and not a drop when he wanted it most. But there was no need to fight the blackness threatening to engulf him. No more to be done. No bloodshed, save his own. Kate safe, Kate . . .

He jerked himself upright; then slid from the saddle and led his horse to the side of the road, to let the marching column pass. The night was reduced to the thud of feet and the throbbing of his injured cheek.

Jesse's voice boomed in his ear.

"Here she is, Mr. Carryll."

Kate stumbled into his arms and laid her head on his shoulder. She whispered brokenly, "Oh, Richard, I was so afraid. I thought you had forsaken me."

He held her close, aware of her trembling, the coldness of her hands.

"Never. I swear it, Kate."

Suddenly she drew away from him, staring at the dark stain on her fingers.

"Richard, you are injured. Oh, my dearest—"

"It is nothing. Kate, listen to me—"

But beyond her, he saw a sight which cut short his words. Two men were lifting Jamie to the ground; the baronet's body still hung limply across the horse.

Kate turned Richard's head so that the moonlight fell upon his cheek. He heard her gasp. Impatiently he shook himself free of her hand.

" 'Tis but a flesh wound. There is no time to attend to it now. I still háve work to do. But first —what of yourself? Silas said you had been hurt."

"Only my ankle. 'Tis not serious. But you have lost much blood. You must—"

He put her from him. "Let me be. The danger is not over. We still have upon our hands, a load of contraband and—a body."

Jamie's voice came out of the shadows, in croaky jerks. "I—I didn't mean to kill him, sir. But he was going to harm Mistress Hardham. I had to stop him." He gulped loudly. "I heard Willy, telling how the gibbets creaked. You'll not let them hang me, sir?"

"Have we not just saved you? Kate, look to the boy, while I think what must be done."

She started to protest. But he turned from her and walked a few paces apart, the better to plan carefully. He looked back once. She was sitting on the bank, her arm around Jamie's shoulders, while big Jesse stood guard above them. With all his heart Richard longed to hold her, to declare his love. But first he must ensure her safety. The militia would give them no more trouble at present. But someone would come to investigate, and there must be no trace of this night's deeds.

Clearly, step by step, he worked out his plan, while the men waited impatiently under the trees. Then, when he rejoined them, they rode a silent cavalcade, towards the inlet. Kate rested against Richard, silent and content, conscious of the strength in the arms which held her, aware of the determined lift of his chin. At the road to the village he gave her into Silas's care and bade the shepherd take her and Jamie safely to her cottage.

The habit of years made her utter a last protest. "But, Richard, I do not want—"

"You will do as I say," he ordered quietly. "Though you have saved us this night, you will take no more part in what is the business of men."

She wanted to ask what action he intended; to be sure he had not overlooked some small detail which might betray them. She bit her lip to hold back the questions, the warnings. With a gesture totally feminine, she touched his sleeve.

"You—you will come back to me, Richard?"

He raised her fingers to his lips.

"I will come back. That is a promise only death can break."

The sky continued to be in league with the smugglers. Towering, inky clouds banked up in the west, promising rain. No more moonbeams searched out the actions of the men who moved quietly, purposefully, to carry out Richard's orders.

To the village carpenter he allotted the task of burning Jamie's crutch and fashioning him a new one the next day. He ordered Matthew to wash the telltale stains from Sir Henry's horse, to break a stirrup leather, replace the pistol in its holster, and wrench the saddle to one side. The ostler gave the startled creature a thwack on its flank and sent it cantering along the road to the village. He dropped the stirrup beside the sea wall. A few feet away he laid the baronet's dented tricorne and his whip. He flung the dead man's wig, bloodstained and bedraggled, to rest amongst the reeds.

When all was done, Richard nodded his approval. With a glance at the sky, he remarked, "By the time those clouds have emptied, they will have wiped out any stains left upon the road where the —where he died. Where are the kegs we had time to unload?"

"Hidden beneath the gorse yonder," Jesse answered.

"They must be sunk."

"With ropes attached, so that we may recover them later?"

"Certainly not. In deep water."

The men raised protesting voices. Richard tapped his riding whip impatiently against his boot.

"In deep water, I said. Are you so anxious to be transported for life, for a few litres of brandy? Get them away at once. To you, Jesse, I leave the—other matter."

His head ached. Every so often he felt his senses reeling. But now, calling on a strength of body and mind he never thought to possess, he remained master of himself and the men.

He waited, listening for the slightest sound from the direction of the village, as the ponies moved off to fetch the hidden barrels. He heard the lap of water as a boat received its burden, the ripple along the mudbank as it pulled away. The faint creak of thole-pins, the splash of muffled oars, each sound heightened by his anxious ears, faded. The silence and the darkness closed around him.

His mind followed the passage of the boat—out of the inlet, into the deep water of the central channel. He saw with his inward eye, the fisherman holding the craft steady, while Jesse's strong arms lifted up its cargo. Instinctively, he closed his eyes at the moment when the turbid water of the estuary closed over the body of Sir Henry Glynde.

The band of freetraders dispersed. There were no jokes as they parted this night. Richard, his body bruised and weary, his cheek throbbing, made his way towards the village, his one thought to reach Kate. He had checked, he thought, every detail. All now depended on the officer of militia, on Sir Thomas Martineau, and the ability of the men to hold their tongues. Of the latter, he had little doubt, since they had practised the art for years. But of the reaction of the old and failing magistrate, he could not be sure.

He paused at the inn to bid goodnight to Jesse and Matthew. The sight of these two, leading their horses to the stables, brought to mind a remark Kate had made.

"It was done with only two men, Jesse and the ostler from the inn."

Richard jerked upright, so that his horse stumbled.

"Jesse! A word with you. I understand you both stowed a number of kegs in Miss Hardham's loft. They are still there?"

"Yes, sir."

Richard swore softly. "So! Of all the village, the one still in danger is the girl who saved us this night."

Jesse shuffled his feet, staring at the ground. "I forgot, Mr. Carryll."

"You will come with me, both of you."

They tethered their horses and walked behind him along the narrow street. Dismounting, Richard clutched a stirrup leather to save himself falling. He tapped upon the window pane.

The door opened a fraction.

"Kate? It is only I, and two of the men."

She opened wide the door, took his arm as he stumbled on the step.

He stood swaying, staring round the candlelit room. Beside the fire sat Judith, white-faced, her body tense. On the stool at her feet was Jonathan, holding her hands.

Richard turned to Kate. She had changed her dress, combed her dishevelled hair. Her face was flushed, with a fiery weal where a bramble had torn her cheek. Only a few nights ago in this room, he had slapped her face. Her anger had lasted no more than a moment. She had smiled at him, and offered him that same cheek to kiss.

She stood before him now, with the same light in her eyes, the same air of expectancy.

Oblivious of the others, of everything save that all misunderstanding was over, that they were closer than they had ever been, he took a step towards her.

He saw her joy turn to horror. Stunned, he drew back. She loosed his arm, moved swiftly past him. She cried out as she put her weight on her injured ankle, and stumbled against him.

The cry broke his trance. He turned, saw Matthew crouched, knife in hand. Jonathan leapt to his feet, his back to the fireplace, escape impossible.

"So it was you who betrayed us," the ostler muttered. "I knew we were fools to trust naught but a woman's instinct. This time there'll be no such madness."

"Matthew, stop! It was he who saved us!" Kate exclaimed.

210

The man's lips curled in contempt. The knife blade gleamed in the candle-light.

Judith's hands groped helplessly, while she called to Kate for protection. Jesse appeared in the doorway, staring from one to the other. As he started to speak, Richard held up his hand.

"You heard what Miss Hardham said, Matthew. It is true. This young man came to warn us."

The ostler's eyes narrowed. "If you believe that, you are as soft as she is, Mr. Carryll. He came to make sure *she* was in the trap."

Richard passed a hand across his brow. "I am too weary to argue with you. Put down that knife."

"I'll not. Its place is under this fellow's ribs."

Judith stumbling over the stool, fell to the floor. As Jonathan stooped to raise her, the ostler moved forward, baring his teeth.

Kate gasped. She turned to Richard, speaking his name in urgent appeal.

In a voice he scarcely recognised as his own, he demanded, "Will you obey me?"

The man shook his head, never taking his eye from his victim.

Flinging off Kate's arm, Richard strode forward. With all his remaining strength, he brought his riding whip down on Matthew's wrist. The man yelped; the knife spun through the air.

"Now, you will complete the task for which you came here—which was not murder. There has been sufficient bloodshed this night. But I will spill yours if you do not carry out my orders."

Clutching his wrist, the ostler, shamefaced, retreated up the stairs. Jesse, grinning, murmured some words of approval, and went to fetch the ladder.

Within ten minutes the kegs were carried down. Richard stood at the quayside as they were loaded into a fisherman's boat and dumped overboard in deep water. Only then did he relax.

Kate, in her doorway, awaited his return. He walked towads her with as firm a step as he could manage, his shoulders pulled back, his head high. His weary mind yet recalled some words he had read in Pope's *Essay on Man*: "One self-approving hour whole years outweighs."

Kate held out her hands, drew him inside the cottage. He found himself alone with her at last. Silently, he looked deep into her eyes, while he sought for the words which would tell her all his thoughts.

But now he was utterly spent. He felt her arms encircle him, heard her voice, warm and comforting. His aching head found its resting-place against her breast, and he knew there was no need of words, of explanations.

He could, without shame now, seek solace at her hands, since this night he had shown himself the man she had always believed him to be.

Yet still there was one thing left undone. Drawing out the gold cross, he raised it to his lips.

"If—if you will take this back, Kate, I swear to love you all my life."

The thin chain glinted as it hung above her cupped hand. But, releasing him, she withdrew her hand and bent her head. With fingers which seemed to him as clumsy as a boy's, he fastened the clasp beneath the hair at the nape of her neck.

She raised her eyes, and behind the joy which shone in them he read a question. But now he knew the words for which she still waited.

"Katharine, my only love, I ask you solemnly to be my wife."

Then he understood what she had meant when she had spoken of each day breaking in a new wonder. For in her face was the glory of a thousand dawns, and in her whispered words the sweet sigh of a summer breeze.

The weariness of his body forgotten, the throbbing of his cheek an unreality, he gazed for a moment longer on the radiance suddenly revealed to him. Then he entered with her a world of which he had only dreamed.

At sight of the carriage drawn up before the entrance to Falcon Grange, Richard reined in his horse. An aged footman stood beside the horses; an even more ancient coachman drowsed on the box. Only one man in the district drove out in such a decrepit coach with servants as old and stiff-jointed as himself—Sir Thomas Martineau.

Richard hesitated. Then, straightening his shoulders, he rode up to the house. His face was impassive as he gave his mare into the charge of the groom, and heard his name announced.

He was received in the drawing-room, since no longer need Arabella endure the lofty, cheerless hall. She greeted him with an abstracted air. Yet he sensed that her air of tragedy was adopted for convention's sake. Her voice held warmth as she presented him to her Aunt Maria.

He was confronted by a woman dressed, albeit in heavy mourning, in the height of London fashion, her high-piled hair topped by a ridiculous frothy lace cap. He found himself being carefully studied from head to toe. He saw the quizzical

213

raising of her eyebrows as she glanced at Arabella, and knew himself dismissed as an unfashionable country fellow.

But now the only effect was to cause him an inward smile. Far more important was his reception by Sir Thomas.

The old magistrate, breathing heavily, excused himself from rising as Richard bowed before him. "You've come, like me, to offer your condolences, Mr. Carryll?" he suggested in a thin, whistling voice. "A sad affair."

Arabella's aunt exclaimed impatiently, "It was no more than my brother-in-law could expect, sir. Always prying and poking into other people's lives, looking for trouble. He found no happiness in his own life, nor gave any. 'Tis to be hoped he'll fare better in the next world."

"Quite, quite. A bad end, though, for a gentleman—undignified."

Richard ventured an inquiry. "You are persuaded, sir, and you, Miss Glynde, that Sir Henry was killed by—by a fall from his horse?"

Arabella raised her brows. "Pray what else should we surmise? The animal returned riderless to the stable, the saddle askew, a stirrup leather broken. Our second footman reported that from his bedroom window he saw my father ride down the drive, near midnight and alone. You know the result of the search—his hat and whip by the wall, his wig in the mud, and now—now that his body has been recovered, with—I am informed—a head wound such as could be caused by being thrown on to the sea wall—"

She lowered her eyes, clasped her hands in her

lap. Richard said quickly. "Do not distress your-self, ma'am. We are all so—"

She raised her hand. "No, Mr. Carryll, pray do not perjure yourself by uttering words which are not true. You are no more sorry than—than the villagers are, at his death. You may perchance be shocked at the nature of it. But, as my aunt re-marked, my father was not one to—to shirk his duty for fear of the consequences."

"You believe then, he was engaged on—?"

Sir Thomas, leaning forward with hand cupped to ear, broke in, "Smoking out the freetraders? Of course he was. Kept plaguing me to support him. Importunate fellow; didn't really care for him. We lived very comfortably here until he came, y'know. Liked his brother better—gay fellow, Charles. I could tell you—"

Richard, intercepting an exchange of embarrassed glances between Arabella and her aunt, remarked, "You were saying, sir, that Sir Henry—"

"Ah, yes. Getting old, y'know, lose the thread. You must pardon me. Yes, the fellow seemed cer-tain he'd enough evidence to call in the militia. Gave me no peace until I set the wheels rolling."

Arabella jerked up her head. "But—I understood my father was alone that night."

"Probably was, ma'am. I told him, can't rely on the militia, y'know, nor the excisemen. Why, our local volunteers let themselves be bested only last week. Story goes, they'd taken some prisoners—caught red-handed, with a bale of French silk on each shoulder. And what happened? Two hun-dred of the smugglers, desperate fellows they are too, surrounded the militia and took back their prisoners. Not a shot fired." He tipped up his wig,

215

scratched his head. "No, that's not quite correct. Their officer was wounded, and 'tis said he marked the smugglers' leader."

Richard found three pairs of eyes regarding him. Arabella's were dubious, unbelieving, her aunt's filled with a sudden respect. The pale, watery eyes of old Sir Thomas held an amused inquiry, repeated in his voice.

"See *you've* suffered an injury, Mr. Carryll."

Richard put a hand to his cheek. His face expressionless, he said calmly, " 'Tis but a flesh wound, sir. I was careless when pigeon-shooting. But this officer—he was not gravely injured, I trust?"

"No. Smuggler fellow did but put some shot through his pistol arm."

"The militia will be strengthened now, no doubt —with reinforcements from another district?"

"I think not. They've more important affairs to attend to—I am informed there are serious riots in—"

"Then it will all continue as before," Arabella broke in. "If—if there is indeed smuggling here, it will go on, just as if my father had not come. It was a matter which occupied his mind day and night. Yet, in the end, he was defeated."

Richard turned to her. "I ventured once to remark to you, Miss Glynde, that London ways are not ours. There are certain elements—loyalties— which bind the people of this district, and beyond, in sympathy for the cause of the freetraders. Your father did not understand this. He tried too soon to stamp out a form of—of protest against unpopular laws, which I think by now you must be aware was encouraged by his brother."

"Which brings us back," remarked Arabella's

216

aunt, "to what I have already said—that Henry meddled too deeply, and reaped the consequences."

Something in her tone made Richard glance up quickly. He met her eyes, dark and shrewd.

"You are suggesting, madam—"

"I am suggesting nothing, sir. Both Arabella and I accept my brother-in-law's death as the accident it *apparently* was. The parson will doubtless give us an appropriate address, and there the matter will end. This poor child has had enough to bear. When the time may be considered proper, I shall take her to London with me."

Arabella's lashes flickered and she could not prevent a smile from lighting up her face.

Richard rose. "Sussex will be the poorer for her absence." He bowed to both ladies. "I shall be entirely at your command, if there is any service I can render you during the remainder of your stay here."

Arabella rested her fingers on his arm. He felt now for her only sympathy—that her road back to London should have had to pass through this dark valley.

"It is kind of you, Mr. Carryll. But I have always believed you kind. Indeed, but for your friendship, I should have been very unhappy here."

He bowed again, raising her hand to his lips. She said, so softly the words reached only his ears, "It would not have done, you know, for either of us to be—pinioned."

He helped the old magistrate to his feet, supported him to the door. In the drive, Sir Thomas turned to Richard.

"Not so many years ago, y'know, there were smugglers in these parts who had the audacity to leave

217

a keg of spirits in my hay loft. Sir Henry should have cultivated a taste for French brandy. He'd be alive now if he had."

Richard looked deep into the misted eyes, interpreting their message.

"You leave your stable doors unlocked at night, sir?"

"I do. I'm an easy-going man, Mr. Carryll. With the decline of one's physical faculties, a quiet, undisturbed life becomes most desirable. At your age, of course, a scratch on the cheek from—from pigeon-shooting, I think you said—is to be considered a badge of manhood. A scar increases your prestige with the ladies, too, I found. You a man for the ladies?"

"I think not, sir. At least, I—" Flushing, he added, "I shall be marrying, in a few weeks time."

Sir Thomas paused, his foot on the carriage step. "Splendid! That fine wench who keeps the village school?"

"Miss Hardham, sir, yes."

The old man chuckled. "Heard Charles talk of her, often. Said she made him wish he were younger. She'll make you a good wife—bring some life into that quiet house of yours, give you a quiverful of lusty children. Make the most of youth, Mr. Carryll, it passes all too soon."

Wheezing, he climbed the steps and entered his carriage. From his seat, he called down, "I'll drink your health, the day I find a keg of spirits in my hayloft."

Richard, rising from his bow as the coach moved off, saw, unmistakably, the old man wink.

14

Leaves, russet and gold, drifted down to lie in the angle of a gable, or float upon the dark water of the lake. Under the sky, crackling with stars, the thin mist weaved fantastic shapes beneath the elms, over the stubble fields.

Kate, standing beside Richard on the terrace of the Manor, clutched her cloak more tightly around her, and sought his hand.

"It will be cold, waiting for the Frenchman. You have dressed warmly enough?"

"If I don any more clothes, I shall weigh down my horse," he laughed.

"Are you sure Silas has perfected the warning signal?"

"Quite sure. But it will not be needed. For what have we to fear? For weeks now we have been unmolested. If there were the slightest hint of trouble, Sir Thomas Martineau would send me word. All is as quiet as it was before—as it was when Sir Charles was alive. And yet you tremble, Kate."

She laid her head against his shoulder. "Women do tremble at such times."

"You would have me stay with you?"

She jerked upright. "Indeed, no. I have not grown that weak."

"Do not wait up for me. I ride to the Chicester caves tonight."

"Think you I could lie abed on the night of a run? Judith will keep me company, chattering of Jonathan. He goes with you?"

"Yes. Even Matthew now accepts the fact that it was he who saved us in the first instance—that night—by bringing you warning. I shall be sorry when Jonathan leaves to join his uncle; he is an excellent footman."

"I shall miss Judith when she joins him. But they will not be so far away that we cannot visit. Though —" She paused, frowning. "Perhaps you would not consider it seemly for me—to call upon your former footman."

He took her hand, raised it to his lips. "Oh, Kate, Kate!"

Her frown deepened. "You are laughing at me."

"Forgive me, dearest. But this new Katharine who seeks to mould herself on conventional lines, is a stranger to me."

"But, Richard, as your wife, I—"

He drew her to him. "As my wife, you are perfect. I told you once before, I would have you none other than you are."

"You did not mean it then."

"I mean it now—with all my heart. Will you not believe me—and cease trying to become like Arabella?"

She drew away from him, moving along the terrace in a fair imitation of Arabella's glide; then returned swiftly to his arms.

"It is no use," she laughed. "I am not fair or blue-eyed, or—elegant."

"Nor do I wish you that way, or any different, now or ever."

"Not even when—?"

"No," he answered sharply. "I have known more happiness in these four months of our marriage than in my whole life. Do you not know that I want

220

my son to share that happiness—that I want the laughter of my children to echo in my home, instead of the sighs with which I filled it in my youth? It is from you, as you are, have always been, that they will have the gift of laughter."

Her arms circled his neck, drew down his head.

"And from their father?" she whispered. "What will they have from him?"

When he remained silent, she answered for him. "I will tell you, my love. They will inherit kindness and gentleness and patience. But above all these, he will teach them—courage."

He sought to argue. But she put a hand over his mouth.

"No. Richard. I will no longer hear your protests. For now, since you have proved yourself, you do not believe them to be true."

He held her close, kissed her with a passion which made even this short parting painful.

They drew apart as Jamie appeared, leading Richard's horse. The boy held himself upright now. His bones were no longer like the spars of a ship; his face was tanned with long hours of sunshine absorbed as he tended the Manor garden.

He held the animal's head as Richard mounted. Yielding up the reins, he said, "Do not be anxious about Mrs. Carryll, sir. I will guard her from all harm while you are absent."

Kate put an arm around the boy's shoulders. "We know you will, Jamie. We know that—only too well."

Richard nodded, smiling down at them. Jonathan came from the stables to join him.

Kate laid a hand on Richard's knee. "Take care, my love. However safe you think it, there may still

221

be—hazards. Oh, I had almost forgot. Take this."

He peered at the fragment of green she gave him. "A four-leaved clover. Oh, Kate, you are incorrigible!"

"It can do you no harm, and—"

"Very well. I will cherish it as if it were gold. But I have already my magic cloak, which is the best protection any man could wish."

"What nonsense is this? What magic cloak?"

He bent to kiss her once again. "A cloak which you weave more closely every day—the cloak of love."

She stood, listening to the thud of hooves down the drive. When the sound had died away, she found herself alone. Jamie had withdrawn to the shadows, awaiting the moment when she would call him to his books, for he could not be persuaded to go to bed until Richard returned from a run.

She crossed the terrace and leaned on the balustrade, shivering a little in the night's chill.

In the stillness, she heard Richard's mare, cantering round the meadow in frustration at being left behind. Overhead a faint whirr of wings betrayed a flight of duck, returning to winter on the estuary. The scent of newly turned earth filled the air, earth which had received the seed that would bring forth green shoots in the spring as she, at the time of blossom, of birdsong, would welcome the new life now sheltered within her.

In the distance, through the trees, she caught a glimpse of a light. It winked three times. Anxiously she watched, staring into the darkness. The light appeared again, swaying gently to the lift of the Frenchman's lugger.

Sighing with relief, Kate turned and walked

back across the terrace. With surprise she realised she had not felt any tingle of excitement up her spine, nor any urge to don men's clothes and join the freetraders.

Under the weathered grey porch of the Manor, she paused. Then, taking a deep breath of contentment, she entered her home, wherein lay her real adventure, and complete fulfilment.

THE ROMANTIC NOVELS OF
Georgette Heyer
All just 75c

02601	April Lady
02891	Arabella
04832	Bath Tangle
11000	A Civil Contract
11771	Cotillion
24825	The Foundling
25300	Friday's Child
30241	The Grand Sophy
69891	The Quiet Gentleman
71301	The Reluctant Widow
77832	Sprig Muslin
79351	Sylvester Or, the Wicked Uncle
81640	The Toll Gate
84665	The Unknown Ajax
86111	Venetia

Available wherever paperbacks are sold or use this coupon.